KU-099-053

'You're not following doctor's orders,' Harry murmured.

Letting down her guard a little, she sighed. 'My first mistake here.'

'It won't be your last...'

'Thanks a lot!' The bristle was back, with bells on.

'Don't keep a running tally,' he advised, staying calm.

'Why, you'll do that for me?' The tone was sweet, but he didn't miss the bite behind it.

'Rebecca...'

'Harry...' She mimicked his heavy tone, then lifted her chin. 'Your advice is perfectly sound, I admit.'

'Wow! That's a first,' he muttered.

After living in the USA for nearly eight years, **Lilian Darcy** is back in her native Australia with her American historian husband and their three young children. More than ever, writing is a treat for her now, looked forward to and luxuriated in like a hot bath after a hard day. She likes to create modern heroes and heroines with good doses of zest and humour in their make-up, and relishes the opportunity that the medical series gives her for dealing with genuine, gripping drama in romance and in daily life. She finds research fascinating too—everything from attacking learned medical tomes to spending a day in a maternity ward.

Recent titles by the same author:

TOMORROW'S CHILD
WANTING DR WILDE
MIRACLE BABY*
MAKING BABIES*

* linked titles

HER PASSION
FOR DR JONES

BY
LILIAN DARCY

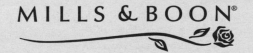

MILLS & BOON®

DID YOU PURCHASE THIS BOOK WITHOUT A COVER?

If you did, you should be aware it is **stolen property** as it was reported *unsold and destroyed* by a retailer. Neither the author nor the publisher has received any payment for this book.

All the characters in this book have no existence outside the imagination of the author, and have no relation whatsoever to anyone bearing the same name or names. They are not even distantly inspired by any individual known or unknown to the author, and all the incidents are pure invention.

All Rights Reserved including the right of reproduction in whole or in part in any form. This edition is published by arrangement with Harlequin Enterprises II B.V. The text of this publication or any part thereof may not be reproduced or transmitted in any form or by any means, electronic or mechanical, including photocopying, recording, storage in an information retrieval system, or otherwise, without the written permission of the publisher.

This book is sold subject to the condition that it shall not, by way of trade or otherwise, be lent, resold, hired out or otherwise circulated without the prior consent of the publisher in any form of binding or cover other than that in which it is published and without a similar condition including this condition being imposed on the subsequent purchaser.

MILLS & BOON and MILLS & BOON with the Rose Device are registered trademarks of the publisher.

*First published in Great Britain 1999
Harlequin Mills & Boon Limited,
Eton House, 18-24 Paradise Road, Richmond, Surrey TW9 1SR*

© Lilian Darcy 1999

ISBN 0 263 81791 1

*Set in Times Roman 10 on 11½ pt.
03-9909-56518-D*

*Printed and bound in Spain
by Litografía Rosés S.A., Barcelona*

CHAPTER ONE

IN CENTENNIAL PARK, the early morning joggers were still jogging, the cyclists were still cycling and there came the regular rhythm of a horse's hooves flying by at an impressive canter. Opposite the park, a row of stately old houses basked in the sunshine of a perfect Sydney spring morning. It was the sort of morning, Dr Harrison Jones considered, feeling energy and life surging in him like sap rising in a tree, when there'd have to be something wrong with any human being who actually *wanted* to be indoors.

Cats, it seemed, felt differently. As Harry walked up the path of attractively worn herringbone brick to his senior partner's door, he could see a tubby old black and white puss, lifting its head and miaowing impatiently, persistently and very loudly to be let in.

At his approach, the cat fled into a huge hydrangea bush, then a second later a ringing, musical voice scolded loudly from behind the door, 'Go round to the *back* door, you lazy thing!'

Before the sentence had been completed, the door opened a little more than cat-width to reveal a quite startling display of long female legs, supple female arms and a curvaceous female torso, topped by a frenzied halo of dark hair. This blue-eyed vision was clad only in a very large, very fluffy and very loosely draped pink towel.

She looked Harry full in the face for one moment and shrieked impressively, then the door slammed shut again.

Harry assessed the situation. He assumed that the reprimand about the back door had not been addressed to him. It therefore seemed best to wait. In a few moments, Rebecca Irwin—that amazing vision had to be Rebecca Irwin—would summon her father to answer the door, then unobtrusively retire to her own room, and the episode of the pink towel need not be mentioned by anyone.

This was such an eminently discreet solution to a moment of mild, shared embarrassment that he was startled when the door opened again almost at once, man-width this time.

'Sorry,' said Dr Rebecca Irwin with a dazzling smile. 'I wasn't talking to you.' The pink towel was pulled around her a little more tightly now, and its end was tucked in firmly between her rounded and very feminine breasts. One as-if-carelessly splayed hand made quite sure it stayed there. The other hand loitered nonchalantly by her long, smooth thighs, where the towel came to an abrupt end, to forestall any possibility of a revealing split opening up.

'I hoped you weren't,' Harry responded mildly, hoping he sounded more suave and in control than he felt.

'It was the cat.'

'Yes, I heard him miaowing.'

'Where's he got to now, I wonder?'

'He dived off into the bushes when I came up the steps.'

'Oh, he's an awful old wuss, bless him. He has a perfectly functional cat door round the back.'

'So I understand.'

There was a strangled quality to Harry's words, and he wasn't surprised when she misinterpreted them. 'You didn't really think I meant—?'

'Me?' he cut in quickly. 'No. No, I knew exactly who you meant. It's fine.'

'Good. I know who you are, of course.' Her face fell in momentary horror. 'At least, I hope... Harrison, right?'

'Harry,' he urged.

She was clearly relieved. 'Yes, so please come in. Dad's on the phone to the garage now. The mechanic seems to have a lot to say, unfortunately, which doesn't bode well for the state of Dad's car.'

'Then it might not be fixed today?'

He had followed her into the house. She really did carry off the pink towel ensemble admirably. With those long legs, those ivory shoulders and that stormcloud of hair, she could have been a model on a Paris catwalk, except that he couldn't imagine a model's look of sulky and supercilious boredom ever crossing Rebecca Irwin's vibrantly mobile face.

'Dad'll have a fit if it's not,' she said over her shoulder, still talking about Marshall's car. 'He doesn't often need it during the day, but Georgina Bennett is due for her weekly home visit at lunchtime, and—'

'I can see Georgina,' Harry answered. 'And I can drop Marshall home here after work.'

'Well, I know, but you know Dad.' She said it with a fond, protective lilt. 'He finds it so hard to delegate.'

She turned. They'd entered a spacious living-room where two bay windows let the sunshine in to fall upon an untidy group of light-thirsty potted plants. The furnishings were comfortable rather than luxurious. Grey marble and rust-coloured tiles surrounded an original turn-of-the-century fireplace. Worn but well-polished wood framed glass-fronted built-in bookcases.

There was a thick paperback novel tossed carelessly onto the floral fabric seat of a couch, and a pair of bright, strappy sandals had been kicked under the glass-topped coffee-table. Harry had been in Marshall Irwin's home before and had enjoyed the atmosphere, but there was something even more welcoming about the place today.

'Sit down while you wait,' Rebecca invited. 'Um...can I get you anything? Coffee?'

'No, thanks. I'm fine.'

'I'm sure he won't be long. But if you'll excuse me, I've got...er...things to do.'

She gave another scintillating smile and waved her hand vaguely, then clapped it quickly back to her chest as the towel threatened to descend. The look of alarm on her face came and went in less than a second.

'Please, don't let me keep you,' he said gravely as he firmly quelled the desire to speculate on how she'd carry it off if the towel *did* drop. Superbly, he was sure. He couldn't resist adding, 'You look stunning in pink, by the way.'

There was a tiny beat of silence before her reply, and her face changed as if she might have been angry. 'Thanks, I'll keep that in mind next time I'm shopping,' she said lightly instead.

A moment later she had left the room and he heard her bare feet padding up the wooden stairs. There came the sound of a door opening and closing, then silence.

Sinking into the giving cushions of the couch, the very capable, very controlled Dr Harrison Jones buried his head in his hands and groaned aloud. He didn't normally come out with suggestive comments like that to women he hardly knew. He didn't normally feel his body crawling with heat the moment he laid eyes on an expanse of female skin. And to have it happen with Rebecca Irwin, of all people...

This was going to be a disaster!

It had been a done deal when he'd joined the practice just on six months ago. Marshall's daughter, Rebecca, would be coming on board in September, after finishing her six-month, hospital-based obstetrics diploma course in the middle of the year, then taking a two-month locum position to help out a friend.

Even then, faint alarm bells had rung. Marsh's pride in his daughter stuck out a mile. His love, too. That was great, of course. Normal. Wonderful. But would it make for a workable professional relationship when she was joining the practice so soon after qualifying? Harry had his doubts. She was only twenty-seven years old, against his own thirty-four.

He'd pushed those doubts aside, however, as he'd spent time adjusting to Marshall's routines and attitudes. The polished fifty-year-old was competent and caring, as Harry had soon realised, and they worked together better than he'd dared to hope.

Marsh was keen to try new ideas, always listened and obviously appreciated a quality in Harry which he himself thought of as a strength but which he knew some would consider a liability—his invariable willingness to speak his mind.

'We can't function as a team,' Marsh had said more than once to Harry and to Grace Gaines, the third practice partner, 'if we don't air problems and opinions honestly. That's not to say that tact and sensitivity go out the window. But I value frankness and I want it in my practice.'

Those hadn't been just words either, Harry had discovered. Grace had confirmed it, too.

'With old Dr Rattigan,' she had told Harry several months ago, 'we were always pussy-footing around, prevaricating to patients and being so "diplomatic" to the office staff that they sometimes didn't have a clue whether they'd been given a compliment or a reprimand. Marshall used to have to go to hideous lengths sometimes to keep to his own ideas. He was forced to be very protective of his territory, and he hated it. Now that Alan has retired, it's like a breath of fresh air.'

A breath of fresh air. That was how Rebecca Irwin seemed to Harry. A breath of fresh spring air. Someone who could shriek at being caught in a towel one minute, then handle it with casual poise the next. She was delightful. Clever. Gorgeous. Sparkling.

And dead wrong about her father not being able to delegate. Being able to delegate now after Alan Rattigan's overdue retirement, that was something Marshall Irwin relished openly.

So it's just as I feared, Harry thought. They're both going to have ingrained, outdated opinions about each other. They're going to be so eager for it to work out well that they'll be falling over themselves. And so will I! But she's had so little opportunity to look at alternatives to how her dad works, so little practical experience other than what she's going to get here with him. It's not good…not good. And at some point very soon, Marsh is going to want my opinion on the whole thing. She's starting on Monday. What can I tell him?

One quite impossible thing sprang immediately to mind—'I hadn't expected your daughter to be quite so attractive.'

It was the fault of the pink towel, of course. One didn't usually encounter one's new junior practice partner for the first time outfitted in such a manner. If they'd met at the surgery, and she'd been wearing a nice, businesslike suit in any colour but pink—with a white coat on top, perhaps—he wouldn't have noticed those ivory legs and shoulders, and that hair so dynamic it looked like a swarm of dark bees clustering round her well-shaped head. He wouldn't have noticed the curves of her figure, exaggerated by the thick, tightly pulled towelling.

He still would have noticed her eyes, though. They were as blue as the Pacific Ocean on a sunny spring day.

This was going to be a total, unmitigated disaster…

Upstairs, in her old bedroom, Rebecca was still smiling. Wryly.

'So, where's my Oscar?' she said aloud to the swing-mirror on top of her dressing-table. 'Wasn't that an award-winning performance?' She still felt quite fluttery, as if recovering from stage fright.

The only genuine thing about it had been the shriek at the beginning when she'd opened the door to find not dear, lazy old Gus but a laid-back, slightly amused and startlingly good-looking man whom she knew must be Dr Harrison Jones.

Dad had said nothing about what he looked like. Well, why would he? Men, and especially men of her father's generation, just didn't describe people that way. Undoubtedly, Dad had never consciously noticed how utterly virile his practice partner was, with that long, solid torso, muscles which were developed like an athlete's and powerfully broad shoulders. Not to mention thick dark hair that clearly refused to do as it was told, white teeth that emphasised the olive of his skin—or was it the other way around? And glinting dark eyes that looked wickedly able to appreciate a good joke—or an under-clad female.

Actually, the slam that had followed the shriek had been genuine, too.

After that... She'd refused to yelp for Dad while she'd scurried upstairs, bathed in a head-to-toe blush. The only choice had been to brazen it out. Quickly redraping the towel, she'd muttered to herself, 'OK, I'm wearing Donna Karan, and Dr Jones has come for a cocktail.' Then she'd opened the door again.

'And I don't think I could have carried it off any better if I *had* been wearing Donna Karan,' she told the mirror, then laughed, blew out a lungful of air and took several more deep breaths.

Letting the towel fall, she reached for the first pieces of clothing she found—an old T-shirt and sweatpants—and put them on quickly.

Downstairs, she heard her father call, 'We're off now, Becca.' Then came the sound of male footsteps and voices.

'Thanks to me, you're missing your swim this morning, Harry.'

'Don't worry about it...'

Then the door opened and closed again, and she knew she was alone. It was quite a relief, for some reason.

Her thoughts still skittering, she began to wonder about the day. It beckoned delightfully, a last interlude, before starting in the practice which could well be the setting for her entire medical career. Tomorrow she and Dad would be toiling around the car dealerships along Parramatta Road in search of a new car, since her old vehicle hadn't been worth bringing from Melbourne.

But today… Somehow, she felt unusually alive, with all the vibrancy of spring singing in her blood.

'So, I'm afraid you hardly got a chance to see Becca,' Marsh said from the passenger seat of Harry's car as they drove off.

'Er, no,' Harry managed, wondering if there was some humorous intent in the words which he'd entirely failed to detect. He had, in fact, had far more of a chance to see Becca…or a chance to see far more of Becca…than he'd anticipated.

He realised just in time that Marsh wasn't joking at all. He hadn't known anything about the towel. On the phone in the kitchen, he'd heard but not seen his daughter come down the stairs to let in the cat. And her shriek, though remarkably expressive, hadn't been all that loud.

Harry's mind snagged on that nickname, too. Becca. Another danger sign.

'Do you always call her that?' he asked Marshall.

'Call her…? Oh, Becca?' Immediately, the older man winced, and gave a nod of understanding. 'I shouldn't, should I? Not any more.'

'Well, yes, she might feel that it compromises her dignity a little in the professional environment,' Harry agreed carefully, feeling somewhat reassured.

The saving element in this situation was that Marshall was generally so quick on the uptake. If a problem developed, he'd put his finger on it very quickly. He always did.

Except that this was his daughter, his only daughter, which meant that there were no precedents, and a man's normally competent judgement might very easily go flying out the window. Harry suspected that *his* would if he had a daughter like Rebecca.

Changing gear to turn into Anzac Parade, he knew that he wasn't ready to relax yet. Marshall's next words confirmed that his doubts were well founded.

'It's going to be marvellous, having her, though. I'm very

proud that it's what she wanted—to come and work with me. It'll round out the practice nicely. We've got my generalist skills, your sports medicine focus and Rebecca and Grace both taking on obstetric work now that Southshore Hospital is stressing a community-based approach in that area. I'm looking forward very much to having her on board.'

'Yes,' Harry agreed weakly. 'It'll be great.'

The traffic was bad. Marsh hadn't exactly invited him to air his doubts. Now wasn't the time or the place. And yet diplomacy that bordered on dishonesty was not his style. He knew that if Marshall asked him straight out for his real opinion, he'd have to give it. He was relieved when the older man turned the conversation to a couple of difficult patients instead.

I should have known, though, that Marsh was too perceptive to be fobbed off like that, he was forced to conclude just four hours later. They'd had a routine morning, crossing paths several times in the corridor or the reception area between patients. Now it was lunchtime and Harry already had his car keys in his hand, on his way to see Georgina Bennett at home. She depended on a weekly visit for her prescription painkillers, and needed a regular check-up as well.

'The parts are in for the car,' Marshall announced, coming out of his office. 'They say it'll be fixed by five.'

'Better than you hoped this morning.'

'Yes, for a wonder. I'd started to wish I'd driven it the extra distance down to Frank Bennett's back yard. I get the impression when I visit Georgina that they're quite an operation, and that mere grease and oil changes are wasted on them. You're going to see her for me?'

'On my way.'

'Not just yet, Harry, if you don't mind. Let's talk for a bit, first...'

'Sure.' He followed his senior partner's ushering hand through into Marshall's office.

'About Rebecca.'

Harry murmured something noncommittal and sat down opposite Marshall, who'd retreated—if that wasn't too loaded a word—behind his desk. The atmosphere was already a little strained.

Harry found himself examining a container of tongue depressors with unwarranted interest as he waited for Marsh to speak, and then, still waiting, he turned his attention to the proliferation of little stick-on notepads, provided by pharmaceutical reps, piled neatly on one corner of the desk. Although useful, there was something very annoying about them somehow. Now, why *was* that?

But Marsh had gathered his thoughts now. 'You know,' he said slowly, 'I consider myself a pretty competent man...'

'No disagreements there,' Harry answered with a chuckle that didn't quite ring true.

'And yet, where my daughter's concerned, something's different. It started with her mother's death, of course, twelve years ago. Rebecca was heroic then—and from then on. There's no other word for it.'

'I can imagine.'

'She was fifteen, and right in the middle of that stage where they don't want to be seen within half a mile of their parents out in public. But that changed overnight.

'Simon was only ten, and—no, I'm not going to use the cliché. She *wasn't* like a mother to him.'

'No?'

'Instead, she was the most wonderful big sister you can imagine. Joy's death could have scarred us all very badly, but it was Rebecca who kept that from happening. She was too protective of me, of course. Still is.'

'Understandably,' Harry offered.

Then suddenly the grateful father was gone and the experienced senior doctor was back. '*Do* you understand, though, Harry?' Marshall demanded. He leaned forward. 'I got the impression in the car this morning that you weren't entirely happy about Rebecca joining the practice. You've got qualms, and it's my fault that we haven't discussed this earlier. Air them now, please, because you know I won't thank you for dishonesty. You're crucial to the future of this practice, and your opinion is extremely important to me.'

Harry sat forward, too. 'I have got qualms,' he said, his gaze as fixed and serious as his partner's. 'Not about a father and daughter in the same practice as such. A lot of practices work that way. Brother and sister. Married couple. Father and son. And you've told me some of Rebecca's results at university. She's obviously very bright, capable and committed to medicine.'

'But?' Marshall supplied helpfully.

'But,' Harry agreed, then put his elbows on the desk, pressed his fingertips together and took a moment to make sure it came out right.

Toiling around the car dealerships on Parramatta Road with Dad tomorrow? Not any more!

On such a gorgeous day, with all the favourable auspices in place, Rebecca decided that life was too short to spend looking at seven different brands of vehicle when she'd already researched the subject pretty thoroughly in car magazines over the past month or two. She knew what was top of her list, with the right price and the right attributes. She didn't particularly care what colour it came in.

Pink, perhaps, since some people apparently considered she looked good in that colour. She shook her head, grinning, as she washed up the breakfast dishes and thought back on her unusual encounter with Harrison Jones. Probably she ought to be wishing it had never happened. Maybe she ought to be angry with him for teetering on the edge of flirting with her, but somehow it had been almost fun. As long as it wasn't setting a precedent, of course...

But Harrison Jones was not the subject at issue, she reminded herself hastily. The issue was cars.

If she took one for a test drive and liked it in the flesh, so to speak, why not buy it on the spot this morning and save poor Dad from an experience that he'd undoubtedly loathe? In the Irwin family's opinion, no sane person actually *liked* buying a car.

Accordingly, at ten o'clock, after some leisurely housework, she changed from her sweatpants and T-shirt into a smartly styled pale yellow linen suit which positively shouted her car-buying competence and took a taxi to the relevant dealership. She drove out onto Parramatta Road with her brand-new, compact-sized, air-conditioned, dark metallic green toy just on two hours later. The effect of the purchase on her finances was a little painful, but hefty loans were a fact of life these days, for doctors as much as for anyone else.

Almost lunchtime. Traffic building. Dad's practice half an hour away, in a side street within easy walk of Maroubra Beach. I'll go and show off the car, and persuade him to come for a quick take-away by the water!

The practice was quiet when Rebecca arrived. Locked, in fact, with a little sign behind the glass door saying, Back at...' and a clock with red plastic hands, reading 12.45. It was almost that now. Since she had a key, it wasn't a problem in any case.

She let herself in, grinning privately when she envisaged her father's face at the sight of the new car. He might think she'd been somewhat hasty...but he'd be extremely relieved that the dreadful deed had been done, all the same.

Voices came from Dad's office and, still with surprise on her mind, she tiptoed down the corridor—then stopped short.

'Yes, that's exactly my point, Marshall,' came Harrison Jones's deep and slightly scratchy voice, rising with conviction and confidence. 'She's too inexperienced to join a practice in which both you and she have such a strong vested interest in getting on well. It'll make for just the sorts of problems you've told me you so disliked when Alan Rattigan was here. Tactful manoeuvrings and over-concern about hurt feelings, that sort of thing. I'm very happy to hear that you see me as crucial in this practice, and I appreciate that you've asked me to be honest about all this. The bottom line, I have to say, is that I'd have suggested she not join the practice…'

Surprise and the car forgotten, Rebecca fled back down the corridor, ears burning, face flaming, throat tightened, too shocked to stay and hear more. She'd heard enough!

It didn't take much consideration to realise that Dad and Dr Jones were talking about *her*. And it didn't take much interpretation to work out that Harrison Jones was laying down the law.

'"That's exactly my point, Marshall,"' she echoed through gritted teeth. And his point was that he didn't want her here.

She paced the empty waiting-room, fuming, her good feeling about the day quite evaporated.

Empire-building. Taking advantage of Dad. It felt, for some reason, like a huge betrayal. The good feeling about that ridiculous incident with the pink towel stopped tickling the corners of her consciousness and her response to Harry Jones now was boiling anger. She felt, though she knew it was illogical, that he must have deliberately set out to break down her defences this morning. She should have slammed the door in his face and left him there until Dad was ready!

He sees me as a threat, presumably. He knows I won't put up with my father getting bulldozed or manipulated into changes in the practice that he doesn't really want. He must know that with me here, Dad has an ally and a watchdog. Why is Dad *swallowing* this?

Will I confront the man? No, not yet! Let him show his hand a little more first! And let me wait and see what Dad's response is. Perhaps Dad isn't swallowing it at all, and he'll tell Harrison Jones exactly where to get off!

She smiled grimly at the pleasing image of the man skulking from Dad's office with his metaphorical tail between his legs, like a chastened dog.

CHAPTER TWO

'I'D HAVE suggested she not join the practice for a couple more years,' Harry said to his senior partner, leaning forward and meeting Marsh's gaze openly. 'It would have been different if this was a way-station for her, perhaps, but since she does intend to stay...'

'That's what she's told me,' Marshall Irwin answered. 'Look, there's no doubt that Rebecca is over-protective where I'm concerned.'

'And I'm not saying that's a bad thing, Marsh.'

'I know. To be honest, I've needed that at times. That evidence of her love and support.'

'Doesn't anyone?'

'In fact, there was a particularly difficult time about two years ago when I— But, no.' Marshall interrupted himself with a shake of the head. 'That's not something you need to hear about now. You feel if we'd both been more patient about her joining, she'd have come with a firmer foundation of her own experience, and she'd be on a more equal footing here?'

'That's exactly it, yes. I think, for the long haul, you might have made it easier on yourselves, that's all.'

'But since the deed is done?' Marshall asked.

'Tread carefully. We'll all need to. Grace as well.'

'And I should have considered all this eight months ago?'

'You know, I don't think you could have,' Harry answered honestly, after a moment's thought. 'I know how much you've missed her the years she's been in Melbourne, and you knew Simon was heading off to Harvard for his MBA. It's obvious how delighted you are that she wants to work with you. If I had a daughter, I'd feel the same.'

19

'You'd make a good father, Harry.'

Harry waved this aside. 'I'm not sure what sort of a man you'd have to be to say no to her joining the practice straight away,' he continued, 'Because, of course, there'd be a real risk that if she did begin work elsewhere she'd get settled there and the move to this practice would never happen. When I think about it, I'm probably guilty of advising something that, in your circumstances, I wouldn't be able to do myself!' he finished.

'No, don't back down, Harry,' Marshall said. 'You're absolutely right. We're going to need to tread carefully. And me most of all. I'm glad we had this talk.'

'So am I.'

'Look, could I ask for your help? If you could be the one to keep an eye on her, give her any guidance she needs, when the chance comes up.'

'Are you sure, Marsh?'

'After what you've just said, yes. She's bound to need advice at times, and it's likely she'll take it better from a disinterested colleague than from her father. You don't beat about the bush, Harry.'

'So I'm often told!'

'And yet you're tactful.'

'Not always!'

'When it counts. So, will you do that for me?'

'I'd be...honoured, actually,' Harry answered.

'Good, Rebecca couldn't be in better hands.'

They both emerged into the corridor a moment later, well pleased with the exchange. Harry was already thinking about the role that Marshall had just entrusted to him. It was a responsibility, and it might well be a challenge. He'd need to think carefully about how best to handle it. In other words, how to keep his tact to the fore and his bluntness well in check!

Now they found Rebecca herself at the front entrance, her

keys still in her hand. She must only just have arrived. Except that, after he'd walked along to the waiting-room and taken a good look at her, Harry knew she *hadn't* just arrived. She'd been here long enough to overhear their conversation, and she was furious. Hurt, too, perhaps. How much of it had she heard?

Enough, evidently, to bring a bright, unnatural glitter to her dark eyes and a stain of angry pink to her cheeks. Yes, pink again. She looked magnificent, her chin held high to emphasise a strikingly clean, graceful jawline, her hair tossed wildly everywhere. Her anger was only just contained beneath some scintillating chatter to her father about the car she'd just bought, and the only reason Marsh hadn't picked up on her underlying mood himself was that he was half-hypnotised by the sight of the brand-new car keys she was dangling before his vision.

'It was right there in my stars in the newspaper, Dad. "Use your energy to act boldly. Money spent today will be spent well." '

'And you run your life according to a newspaper horoscope these days, do you, Rebecca?' Marshall returned helplessly.

'Well, not quite,' she admitted on a drawl. 'But I knew you'd only said you'd come tomorrow because you thought you *ought* to. You know the idea. Big, strong fathers have to protect timid, frivolous daughters against nasty, unscrupulous car salesmen. But I beat him down by $800, and he even managed to treat me as if I already knew what anti-lock brakes were. Which I actually sort of do. So come and see! It's green, and I *love* it!'

Marsh was laughing. 'You're right. I was dreading the expedition, but, while I might grant you "frivolous" on appropriate occasions, I've not seen "timid" since your first day of kindergarten. By the way, mine'll be fixed by five, they're saying now, so you can come back later and drop me at the garage if you've nothing better to do...'

They left the waiting-room together, and Harry just had time to catch one sizzling hot glance from Rebecca, thrown at him with all the disdain and hostility of a Hollywood star throwing a quick photo opportunity to a paparazzo. Her dark eyes blazed.

Such electric, living anger was evidently contagious. Harry found that he was furious as well.

If she'd heard the whole conversation then she was judging it very unfairly. And if she'd only heard a snatch of it, that was even worse. She had no basis on which to judge it at all. Why hadn't she been up front about it and come into the room to join the debate, challenge him openly, instead of skulking around, eavesdropping? That was cowardly and two-faced and petty. She hadn't struck him as that type. No, he'd instinctively pegged her with far more positive attributes, such as honesty, courage and an almost innocent eagerness for the sheer largeness of life.

He would be quite happy to speak as openly to Rebecca herself about his doubts as he'd spoken to her father. Now they'd got off to a very bad start, and he didn't consider it to be his own fault. Nor did he allow himself to fully examine the second thread of emotion that entwined with his anger.

Disappointment, like a physical knot in his gut. There was no reason at all why he should be disappointed in her apparent lack of courage, and yet he was. Badly. It served him right for leaping to such conclusions on the basis of a couple of dazzling smiles and one pink towel!

Shaking his head ruefully and sighing between clenched teeth, Harry pulled his car keys from his trouser pocket again and set off to see Georgina Bennett, crossing paths with receptionist Deirdre Sullivan in the doorway.

She detected his complex and uncomfortable mood at once and her neat, dark head turned. 'Not a problem, is there, Doctor?'

'Just busy,' he said, then, to deflect attention, he added,

'You've had your hair cut over lunch. Looks great. Very stylish.'

It did, too. He was not adept at or happy about telling lies about such things.

'Oh, thank you, Dr Jones.' She beamed.

He was much calmer by the time he reached the Bennetts' small house of dark red brick. He parked in the street, not wanting to block the driveway, which he knew was used constantly by Frank Bennett and his two adult sons, who ran a car repair and restoration business from their back yard. They'd given Marsh's car a grease and oil change more than once.

A visit to forty-five-year-old Georgina could put anything in perspective. She was wheelchair-bound and chronically ill, with an arthritic form of SLE, known more commonly as lupus. Also, and largely as a consequence of her lupus, she had osteoporosis and non-insulin-dependent diabetes, and it was unlikely that her struggling, swollen body would have a long lifespan.

In some ways, despite the warmth and closeness in the Bennett clan, her death would come as a release. The whole family was growing tired by this time, Georgina most of all.

Harry went round the back, where the blue light of a welder flashed inside a galvanised iron shed. Over on an adjacent concrete slab, he saw a pair of legs sticking out from under another vehicle, and in a tiny, makeshift office—really just an enclosed veranda—he saw Frank Bennett on the phone. Younger son Wayne was the first to spot him, and immediately turned off the welder and came towards him.

'I'll show you in, Dr Jones,' he said. 'Mum's expecting you.' He gestured up to another section of enclosed veranda, where Georgina was sitting in her wheelchair and observing the activity in the back yard. She spent a lot of time this way.

Harry smiled at her and gave a casual salute, then asked Wayne, 'How's she been?'

'Not great. The leg's really bothering her. She hasn't been sleeping.'

Several of Georgina's lumbar and sacral vertebrae were crushed, compressing the sciatic nerve and sending severe shooting pains down her left leg. The arthritic pain and swelling in her joints also caused severe discomfort. For several years, before coming under the regular care of Marshall Irwin and his practice, she had been self-medicating with heavy doses of aspirin. Then she'd begun to haemorrhage severely from the stomach, and had almost died.

After her release from hospital into Marshall's care, he had told her very clearly, 'No more aspirin!'

Now she was on a painkiller that was normally available without prescription, but the doses she required were so heavy that special tablets were used, and she needed a signed prescription for them every week. Writing this script out for her was one of Harry's first duties because she was very concerned that it not be forgotten.

In fact, this was the first thing Georgina said as Harry came into the room. 'Got my script?' Her posture was awkward, and she looked up at him crookedly, with her engaging grin.

'Got a pen?' he returned, grinning back. 'Actually, no, here's one in my other pocket.'

'Want some tea? Wayne'll make it.' She'd been crocheting some colourful rosettes, which she would then stitch together to make a rug. The process was painfully slow and difficult for her, but it kept her busy and gave her an outlet for her mental energy. The patterns she used were intricate and clever.

'I won't, Georgina, if you don't mind,' Harry said. 'I'm running a bit late already. Thanks, though.'

'Well, *I'll* have one! Wayne, there's a boy.' She laid the crochet-work in her lap.

'OK, Mum, I'll put the kettle on.'

While he was doing so, Harry ran through everything else he needed to check on. First, a finger-prick and a check of her blood sugar. The level wasn't great. Too high. She might need an increase in her dose of oral hypoglycaemic agents because, according to Marshall's notes from the past few weeks, this was becoming a consistent pattern. It was the prolonged use of steroids to control her joint swelling which had triggered the diabetic condition, but there was no viable alternative.

Next, he questioned her closely about how she'd been feeling, what she'd been eating and what medicines she'd been taking, and got the guilty confession from her that she'd been having a few aspirin just the past couple of days. 'Only a few, here and there. The other stuff just isn't strong enough, Dr Jones.'

He sympathised, but he had to be tough with her. No aspirin. She didn't need a repeat of the haemorrhaging she'd had before.

'OK,' she answered resignedly. 'Sometimes I think I don't care about all that. But OK…'

He asked her about constipation, too, which was a side-effect of her heavy schedule of painkillers, and they bargained back and forth for a while. He wanted her to be more rigorous about increasing dietary fibre and fluid intake. She argued for a laxative.

'Dr Irwin's always talking about fibre and fluids, and I try, but it's just not enough!'

They compromised on fibre tablets.

'But you *must* take the full glasses of water with them,' he told her. 'Or it'll make things worse!'

'Story of my life.' She smiled, then twisted in her chair and called out, 'Wayne, are you *watching* that kettle? Is that why it's not boiling? Don't you know what they say about watched pots?'

'Don't get your knickers in a twist, Mum. It's coming! Filled it a bit full, that's all.'

'I've got another suggestion for you, Georgina,' Harry said, knowing this one wouldn't be popular either. 'Could you cut down on your tea?'

'Oh…! You doctors!' She pelted him with a purple crocheted rosette.

'I know,' he answered glumly, fielding the rosette and lobbing it back. 'If I were you, I wouldn't like me much either.'

'Oh, I like you all right, and Dr Irwin. Doesn't hurt that you're two of the best-looking blokes I ever get to see—'

'Hey!' Wayne protested, coming in with a mug of tea, garnished with a teabag tag. 'Best-looking? What about me?'

'*Apart* from the three lugs I have to live with, was what I was going to say if you'd let me finish!'

'OK, then,' Wayne growled, with an exaggerated pout. 'Just as well, too!'

So the visit ended on a laugh, even if there was nothing in Georgina's situation that really warranted such a thing. They were a brave, exceptional lot, the Bennetts.

Harry returned the way he had come, past the ten-storey tower of Southshore Hospital, where Grace had obstetric visiting rights—as Rebecca would now—and where he regularly sent patients for orthopaedic surgery, performed by specialists in this field. Then his stomach reminded him that he hadn't had lunch. There was still time. He could grab something from one of the take-away places that fronted the beach just around the corner at the end of the street. He'd eat at his desk.

Harry squeezed into a parking spot just behind a very shiny metallic green car which had pulled up moments earlier, and there was Rebecca climbing out of it and heading for the Asian Noodle House twenty metres along the pavement.

At the sound of his vehicle manoeuvring into the space, she turned with a frown, anxious about the bumper of her new car, and recognised Harry at the wheel—at which point the frown deepened and she turned her back once more. The abrupt, haughty jerk of her lemon-clad shoulders made that living dark hair of hers bounce and swing crazily.

Harry's anger returned in full force. 'You won't get away with turning your back on *me*, Rebecca Irwin!' he muttered as he strode from the car. 'Let's have this out in the open before it gets any worse!'

She was standing at the counter of the Asian take-away when he caught up to her, ordering Singapore noodles and lemon-flavoured mineral water.

'Make that two, please,' he added, though he didn't make the mistake of trying to pay for hers.

She was putting up a bright front again, as she had with her father, still talking about the car. 'I took Dad for a test drive and he approves, but then he needed to get back.' The tone was brittle and too high-pitched. 'He had a couple of special-ists to phone.'

She hadn't managed to sustain the bright front for long. Her tone now implied that if Harry had been a decent doctor who pulled his weight in the practice, *he'd* need to get back to the office to phone specialists, too.

Harry was unruffled by the aspersion. 'I've just come from seeing one of Marsh's patients,' he returned in a conversa-tional tone. 'Georgina Bennett. I think you know of her.'

'Oh. Right. I forgot.' She nodded tightly. He could tell that he'd chastened her, despite her heroic attempt to conceal the fact.

He collected his container of noodles and his mineral water and accompanied Rebecca to the door and beyond, despite her best efforts to march haughtily ahead. 'Let's cross the road and sit on that bench on the grass,' he suggested.

'You've only got ten minutes,' she pointed our tartly.

'Enough,' he said.

'You're a fast eater.'

'I'm a fast talker, too. Now, tell me, Rebecca, how much did you overhear?'

He gave her several points for not pretending to misunderstand. 'I heard quite enough,' she told him, above the swish of the traffic as they waited to cross the road.

'Enough for *what*, exactly?' he challenged.

A gap opened up and they plunged across in tandem. Gritting her teeth, Rebecca accepted the fact that they were going to have to eat together...and that he was going to insist on talking through her hostility openly.

I should have hidden it better, like I managed to do with Dad. I shouldn't have let Harrison see that I was angry.

But she knew she wasn't enough of an actress to perform for him twice in one day. In practising medicine, a doctor often had to disguise his or her feelings. Professionally, Rebecca was adept at it. Personally, she showed what she felt, and what she felt at that moment was oddly complex and painful. For some reason, she actually felt...*bruised*.

They reached the bench and sat down in the spring sun-shine, with the red tile roofs of Sydney behind them and the blue-green waves curling and crashing just fifty yards off. There were surfers in the water, as slick as black seals and as patient as bobbing lobster floats as they waited for the right wave. The beauty of the day seemed to mock her earlier sense of freedom and joy and anticipation.

She put down her noodles. The container was almost too hot to touch, and she was too stirred up to eat. The sight of *him* calmly doing so only made her feel worse.

'Enough to realise that you're empire-building,' she accused crisply, not caring how strongly she stated the case.

'*What?*' He stopped eating too.

'That's the only way I can interpret it. You're afraid of my influence on Dad because you want to monopolise that influ-ence yourself. I heard you say quite clearly that you didn't want me in the practice.'

'That's *not* what I said.'

'You have quite a carrying voice at times, Dr Jones.'

'Nevertheless, it's not what I said. I guess you tuned in

halfway through,' he drawled deliberately, 'And tuned out again as soon as you got to a bit you didn't like.'

She felt as if she'd been slapped. 'You're implying that I was deliberately eavesdropping!'

'Well, weren't you?'

'No! I happened to arrive when the surgery was locked and I wanted to surprise— But why is it me who's on trial here?'

'Because, in my opinion, if you *did* hear something that upset you, you should have made your presence known so we could have had it out then and there.'

'No!' she said again, decisively. 'That's the last thing I'd do. If you and I are going to clash, Harrison, then my father is not going to know about it and is not going to be involved. He doesn't need the added stress. And I'll ask you to respect my wishes on that.'

'I'll respect them if it's so important to you. But I think you're wrong,' he said quietly, trying to lower the temperature of this exchange.

What on earth would Marshall think if he could witness this scene? Less than an hour ago, Harry had promised his senior partner to act as a mentor to Rebecca, if necessary. Now they were shouting at each other!

'I'm not interested in what you think,' she retorted. 'You're only his practice partner. I'm his practice partner *and* his daughter. I know him, I care about him and I *won't* have him distressed or hurt by anything that goes on between us.'

Her blue eyes flashed like the Bennetts' welding equipment.

'Nothing needs to go on at all, Rebecca.' His voice was scratchy with impatience. 'And I think your father is stronger than you seem to believe. But if you want to know what I said to him, it was simply this—that I think we all need to be careful because of your lack of experience. That's not a criticism of you.'

'Oh, really?'

'It's just a fact. Less than six months ago you were still

doing your obstetrics diploma. If Marshall had asked my advice—and these, if I'm remembering rightly, are the exact words I used to him on the subject—I'd have suggested you not join the practice for a couple more years while you got experience elsewhere, under more impartial guidance. That's all.'

Rebecca shifted on the wooden bench and stared out at the ocean, feeling the breeze on her skin like a cool hand. If only it helped! She was speechless. It wasn't pleasant to know that she'd been discussed in this way—like a *commodity*—in theory a capable doctor but with the double minus of being Marshall Irwin's daughter *and* inexperienced. The emotional part of her wanted to insist that it was degrading, unfair, but at heart she knew it wasn't. Harrison was entitled to his opinion, even if that opinion made her so angry she just couldn't *wait* to prove him wrong.

'I'm sorry,' he was saying now with surprising gentleness. 'You're burning.'

He reached out and touched her cheek, almost cupping it in his hand, still very gently, and the coolness of his fingers told her that he was right. Her face felt as if it were on fire.

'It's all right,' she said as his hand fell slowly away.

It almost felt as if it had left a mark, and she felt an odd breathlessness which she at once dismissed as meaningless. Of course she was breathless! They'd just been arguing. It had nothing to do with that powerfully male aura that surrounded him, nothing to do with this sudden awareness of her own very different body. *Absolutely* nothing to do with pink towels!

But his dark eyes were fixed on her as if he'd been shocked at the intensity of the moment, too. They both sat frozen for some seconds in silence, and Rebecca wondered if he was having to fight this treacherous physical pull as much as she was.

'It's good to have it in the open, as you said,' she managed finally, stiffly. 'It's a straight bet now, isn't it? You'll collect if I fail, and I'll collect if I succeed. And succeed in this practice, Harrison, is what I fully intend to do.'

'Damn it! I won't collect anything if you fail, Rebecca,' he answered.

'Really? You strike me as a man who places a lot of value on being proved right.'

'Sometimes, yes,' he agreed with ominous patience. 'But in regard to you, it's not what I want at all, and I have no expectation that it's going to happen.'

'Nice of you to say so!'

'Will you please believe me? I was just…sounding a quiet alarm, that's all.'

'Well, sound away,' she said. 'I'll ignore it, if you don't mind, and just get on with the job.'

'Do that, Rebecca. Do that.'

'And hadn't you better do it, too?' she asked sweetly. 'Get on with your job, that is.'

He at once looked down at his watch, a silver circle on the dark leather strap that braceleted his tanned and hair-streaked wrist. 'Damn!' Springing to his feet, he snapped the lid back on his container of noodles and set off immediately, dropping his plastic fork on the ground before he'd gone more than a few metres.

'Harry, wait, you dropped—' Rebecca began, fighting a laugh. He wasn't *that* late! She was absurdly pleased that her words had had such a dramatic effect. Her whole body tingled with triumph, though why on earth she should want to have any sort of power over him she didn't stop to question.

He waved her aside and didn't let her finish. 'If there's one thing I hate,' he shouted back to her, 'it's starting off behind schedule.'

He was already halfway across the road, timing his weave between the cars with the alert, springy steps of a tennis player. She watched him helplessly, and winced a few moments later as he came within a centimetre—it looked from this distance—of ramming her car as he eased out of the kerb-side parking space.

Oh, wouldn't it have given her perverse satisfaction if she'd been able to yell at him about *that*?

Then, still watching him as he drove down the street and slowed at the corner, she went and picked up the fork he'd dropped. She had an oddly vivid image suddenly of his firm, well-shaped lips closing over the white plastic tines as he'd swallowed the three mouthfuls of lunch that their emotional exchange had permitted him.

'Damn!' She echoed his mild profanity aloud to the seagulls which had begun to stake her out as a potential source of scraps. 'Damn!'

Flicking the fork between her fingers, she was left with the disturbing feeling that she'd reacted far too strongly to her future practice partner just now, in all sorts of ways. She wasn't at all sure why, and still less did she know how to regain the lost ground.

CHAPTER THREE

BY THE following Wednesday, Rebecca was starting to feel as if she had her bet with the disturbing Dr Jones almost won.

Not that he'd acknowledged there *was* a bet, of course. He had been impeccably professional with her for the past two and a half days, and she had returned the favour. Harrison Jones had his good points, she had to concede.

She liked the openness of his laugh, and the occasional piquant cynicism of his humour. She'd noted the tin of Viennese chocolate biscuits he had brought in on Tuesday morning for everyone on staff to enjoy with tea or coffee, and liked what that said about his awareness of the importance of creating small islands of friendship and sharing in the busy practice day.

He exuded a casual, relaxed athleticism, too, which shouldn't have impressed her as she wasn't particularly sporty and certainly wasn't fixated on muscular types. But she'd discovered that he swam almost every morning at nearby Maroubra beach, before coming in to work, and there were often strands of dark hair still curling damply at his neck and even the faint, freshly salty smell of the sea clinging to him when his shower afterwards hadn't been quite thorough enough. Yesterday, she'd had the most idiotic urge to grab a hand towel and finish drying him off properly. And he'd looked so invigorated by his swim that she might have considered taking up the habit, if she hadn't known she'd encounter him in the water.

But if he was under any illusion that he was gaining her complete trust...

'Think again, Dr Jones,' she had muttered yesterday afternoon—just before biting into one of his delectable Viennese biscuits.

And Dad was definitely behaving strangely. He verged on ignoring her most of the time, and Rebecca, who had been prepared to speak to him seriously on the subject of him being over-anxious on her behalf, was now starting to wonder if he had something on his mind. He hadn't asked her once how she was managing, how she was enjoying the work or whether she'd had any sticky diagnoses thus far.

Over dinner last night she had mentioned Dotty Gillespie.

'She was concerned about a lump in her breast. She's been with this practice for years, hasn't she?'

'Yes, but we don't see her very often.' He'd reached for a section of the newspaper and forked in a mouthful of spaghetti.

'I'm pretty sure it's a cyst and nothing to worry about, but I've given her a referral to a specialist.'

'Which one?'

'Dr Warner.'

'Mmm,' was the brief response. 'He's good.'

'Dad?'

'Yes?' An apparently reluctant look upwards from the paper.

'Nothing.'

She hadn't been able to articulate the problem then. Still couldn't. Perhaps there wasn't one. Things were going fine. She'd done the right thing with Dotty Gillespie. After all, she hadn't *wanted* Dad to fuss. And Harry had been very helpful on Monday in giving her a complete run-down on procedures and where things were stored so she couldn't claim to be working in the dark.

Sitting back in her swivel chair at four-twenty on Wednesday afternoon, she seized on the moment of respite which her very brief previous appointment had given her. Little Margaret Hurst, aged three, had only come in for a follow-up check on her right ear, to make sure that her course of oral antibiotics had fully cleared the infection. It had. The examination of the healthy ears and throat had only taken a few minutes.

She'd been a sweetie of a thing, though, blonde and blue-eyed and bossy, energetically curious about everything in Rebecca's office and quite happy to talk very earnestly, with her big eyes fixed on Rebecca, about anything that came into her head. It would have been nice to find out more about what went on in that bright little mind, but Rebecca had sensibly chosen to usher Margaret and her mother out in a timely fashion in order to spend a few minutes catching her breath.

Beyond the closed door of her office she heard the activity which was typical in a family practice like this one. The phone rang. The computer printed out an account. A child cried. Harrison's shoes squeaked on the vinyl tiles as he came past with a patient, talking about the weather. Dad was off this afternoon, as he would be on Wednesdays for the next few weeks.

In total there were now ten people on the staff of the practice, which gave the place a buzz of variety and personal contact. There were the four doctors, who between them held appointment hours between eight-thirty and six, Monday to Friday, with a short break for lunch. Their special interests ranged from sports medicine to obstetrics and asthma, and between them they made regular visits to a local nursing home called Hazel Cleary Lodge. There were four receptionists, Deirdre, Chrissie, Andrea and Bev, all married women in their forties or fifties who worked part time.

A part-time practice nurse, Julie Cummings, came in every morning, but her hours would probably need to increase soon, and a dietitian, Nickie Paulsen, came in on Thursdays to help patients with problems such as cholesterol, weight, diabetes, food allergies and any other medical condition which could restrict or dictate diet.

Most patients in the practice who needed hospitalisation

went to nearby Southshore, which was large enough to cater for everything from cancer surgery to acute psychiatric conditions. The practice also had a close relationship with Southshore Health Centre, attached to the hospital, whose director, Dr Gareth Searle, was an old friend of Dad's.

The health centre had two full-time physiotherapists on the staff so most patients who needed follow-up physio, usually after an initial appointment with Harrison for a muscle, bone or joint problem, were directed there.

The only unknown quantity in the life of the practice at the moment was the large medium- and high-density housing development going up three streets away on several hectares of land that had formerly belonged to the Department of Defence. Some of the new dwellings were occupied already, but the rest of the development was behind schedule.

Since Southshore Health Centre and the practice of Irwin, Gaines, Jones and Irwin were the two medical centres closest to the new housing, the coming increase in local population would swell patient numbers at both places considerably. The only questions were when and by how much.

Dad had already said that Rebecca need not work full time at this stage, and that her workload would build gradually as the patient base increased. She wondered whether she should fill the time with activities, or whether she'd find herself run off her feet in a matter of weeks.

Maybe Dad just wants me at home two days a week to keep the house nice and cook him his meals, she wondered now, smiling at the thought. Hardly surprising if he did, given the standard of his own cooking, and she didn't resent the possibility.

He didn't have a housekeeper. His last experience of one two years ago had ended so badly that Rebecca hadn't urged him to repeat the experiment, despite the resultant scratchy meals and amateurish cleaning by both her father and her brother Simon.

Just thinking about the way Tanya Smith had used him, it made her ache for Dad, and tears pricked behind her eyes. She blinked them angrily away. How could any woman have hurt him like that, so callously, when Mum's death had already hit him so hard twelve years ago? It still made her fiercely angry to think of it, and renewed her determination to protect her father from anyone else who had ulterior motives in their dealings with him.

Like Harrison Jones? she wondered now.

Hearing him go past again, she noted the confidence of his stride and his deep male laugh. Did he want more from this practice than he was admitting to? Like complete control, perhaps. There were people like that in all walks of life, people who sought power purely for the sake of it.

On Monday night, Harry and Dad had stopped to eat out together on their way home. Dad hadn't got in until after ten. A friendly meal? Or a business meeting?

If it had been the latter, neither Grace nor Rebecca had been invited. Grace didn't seem to mind, and it had certainly had the air of an impromptu arrangement. But, then, Grace, who was nearly six months pregnant with her first child, was more eager to get home to her obstetrician husband than to extend her working hours with meetings over dinner.

'I'm not going to sit in here getting paranoid and angry!' Rebecca concluded sensibly aloud. 'I don't normally react like this. It's just because Harry Jones…rubs me up the wrong way.' Somehow that last phrase was very unsatisfactory. It didn't encompass the complexity of her feelings about the man at all.

In any case, it was four-thirty, and time to see her next patient, whom she encountered in the waiting room with Harry. The two of them were engaged in a shameless flirtation.

'I know you must be very disappointed that I didn't want to see *you* today, Dr Jones.'

'Well, yes, I think you've actually broken my heart completely this time, after bruising it so badly a month ago when you told me you'd always preferred red-headed men.'

'Perhaps I was just trying to make you jealous…'

'Well, it worked, Irene, it worked.'

His grin was irresistible, and Rebecca's patient had clearly fallen completely under its spell. She was gurgling with laughter and patting her beautifully coiffed hair with a coy gesture.

'Mrs MacInerney?' Rebecca cut in crisply. Really, Harrison Jones had no business attempting to entrance and captivate every female who crossed his path. It was *highly* inappropriate! The fact that Irene MacInerney was ninety-six years old was no excuse!

'Oh, yes, I'm ready.' A little flustered, she picked up her bag and tapped along the corridor on thin yet steady legs.

Living right next door to the practice, she had been coming here for years and was remarkable for her age. Although she did have a range of medical problems associated with her advanced years—fragile, paper-thin skin, recurrent bronchitis and slightly lowered blood pressure—Rebecca knew she'd probably come in today 'for a check-up' mainly to meet the new doctor on staff.

'What a treasure!' Harry was saying, half under his breath. He was grinning after the small, white-haired figure with a beam of a smile as if he really was half in love with her.

'Do you think you should flirt with patients like that?' Rebecca couldn't help challenging him.

'I don't flirt with patients,' he shot back. 'I flirt with *her*. And *she* always starts it!'

'Hmm!'

'And admit it, Rebecca, she's amazing, isn't she?'

'Well, yes, she is. Absolutely.'

'So there you go!' He turned to call his next patient, leaving Rebecca with heightened colour in her cheeks and feeling as if she'd lost points in a game she shouldn't have started in the first place. Chagrined, she followed Mrs MacInerney down the corridor. The ninety-six-year-old came up with a clean bill of health, although a scrape from a fall six weeks ago was still proving slow to heal. At four forty-five, Rebecca was ready for the next name on her list.

John Morrison, a walk-in with no appointment, had the thin folder that betokened a new patient, Rebecca found when she picked it up from the desk at the back of the reception area and called his name. The tall, thin man in his thirties had been pacing the waiting room restlessly, clearly in severe pain, and as he lurched forward she saw why. His right shoulder was dropped back, making his arm hang at a strange angle, and she realised at once that it was dislocated.

'Can you hurry?' he groaned, twisting his face. 'I'm in bloody agony!'

'I bet!' she answered heartily. 'How long ago did it happen?'

'Must be twenty minutes by now. More! Couldn't drive. A mate dropped me off.'

He sniffed absently and pinched his nostrils together with his left thumb and forefinger. Then he moaned and swore. 'Agony!' he said again.

Under the circumstances, Rebecca didn't bother with a detailed chat about his medical history. She sat him on the examining table, quickly prepared an intravenous injection of a morphine-based drug, swabbed his skin and pushed the needle home. It took effect within thirty seconds, making him look relaxed and rather wobbly. She positioned herself behind him and said, 'OK, now, take a deep breath and try to relax.'

'Very rel— relaxed now, Doctor!'

'Good. OK, here goes.'

She had manipulated a dislocated shoulder before, in Casualty in Melbourne during her internship, but the procedure wasn't always easy and she was holding her own breath even as he released his. This could be hard work.

But, to her relief, the shoulder slipped back with butter-like ease straight away, and she was pleased that she had the technique down so well.

'There!' she said.

'Thanks…'

'Anything else bothering you?' He didn't seem in a hurry to leave but, of course, the drug had slowed him down. He wasn't the type of man to create a good first impression. He needed a shave…and his clothes were rather too dirty to give credence to the idea that his jaw was merely sporting eighties-style designer stubble.

He hesitated, before answering her question, and his look seemed speculative. 'No, nothing else,' he answered finally.

'How did it happen, by the way?'

'What? The shoulder? Oh, I…work on a building site.'

'The new housing development?'

'Housing development, yes, that's the one,' he said vaguely. 'You know, unloading…piles of girders and all that? It just went out.'

He gave a spaced out smile and slid down off the examining table to walk to the door. She picked up his file and followed him down the corridor, about to suggest that he sit in the waiting room for a while until he was feeling less wobbly, but he wasn't waiting. As he slammed the waiting-room door behind him and hurried away down the front steps and along the street towards the beach, his gait weaving, the truth hit her like a bucket of cold water.

'Oh, *hell*!' she snarled, leaning one arm on the high counter at the reception desk.

With her nicely manicured hand resting on the phone she'd just put down, Deirdre was looking at the still-rattling slats of the doorblind.

'I've just given a hefty dose of a morphine-based drug to an addict, haven't I, Deirdre?' Rebecca said to her heavily.

'Looks that way, because *I've* just got off the phone with Ros Reynolds at Southshore Health Centre,' Deirdre answered quietly. She was a trim, efficient worker, and was obviously as frustrated and upset about this as Rebecca. 'She wanted to warn us that there's a man going the rounds with a dislocated shoulder. At Southshore he called himself Joe Morrow. If she'd just rung five minutes sooner...'

'No, I should have seen it, should have taken more time and asked more questions, but that shoulder *was* dislocated and he *was* in pain.'

'It's amazing, the lengths they'll go to, isn't it? Putting his own shoulder out.' Deirdre shook her neatly coiffed head.

'He was taking advantage of an old injury, I expect,' Rebecca answered. 'And he's probably done it so many times that it's no trouble now. It certainly went back in easily enough! Like a well-oiled hinge. I thought I'd done a brilliant job! And then it began to nag at me. It was *too* easy!'

'What's up?' said Harry casually...or *was* it casually? He was strolling up to the desk to collect his next file with all the ease of a man taking a springtime walk in the park, but he must have suspected something was up or he wouldn't have asked, Rebecca concluded.

The waiting-room was filling with the backlog and the late appointments that inevitably built up towards the end of the day. Again, Rebecca felt her colour mounting. By now he must think she spent half her time in a passionate flush! She was enveloped in the unique male scent that he exuded, and had to fight her awareness of it. Did he do this to her *deliberately*, she wondered illogically, as a way of undermining her control and competence?

But she managed to meet his mildly curious look head-on.

'I just got conned,' she said bluntly. No point in trying to pretend.

She told the story briefly, then felt his hand brush her arm. The small, unexpected gesture of support after her instinctive suspicions and her earlier attack on the subject of Mrs MacInerney set the fine hairs of her forearm standing on end and made a tingling connection with nerve-endings in her whole body. She distrusted the intensity of the feeling—more, perhaps, than she distrusted the man himself.

'Don't,' she told him. Surely it *had* to be deliberate, the way he used his touch and his body to distract her!

His face closed up and his hand dropped. 'Sorry,' he said in a wooden tone. 'But, look, don't dwell on the man. You did your job. You saw a medical problem that was causing pain, and you fixed it.'

'I know, but—'

'You did the right thing under the circumstances. So *don't dwell on it*,' he insisted. It sounded like an accusation.

Forgetting about the incident was easier said than done. Harry had already taken his next file and probably dismissed it completely, but Rebecca couldn't help feeling that she'd let Dad down, that a more experienced doctor would have assessed the situation more quickly and fobbed Mr Morrison, a.k.a. Morrow, off with a different, non-addictive drug which would not have encouraged a repeat performance.

Now, though, it was possible that word would get around that the Irwin practice was an easy touch or, even worse, that they turned a blind eye. No doctors liked hard-core addicts in their waiting-room. There was the potential for violence and disruption, and even the modest amount of cash that flowed through the receptionists' cash drawer, between visits to the bank twice a day, might be targeted.

Rebecca knew that she'd slipped up, and it nagged at her like the splinter under a seven-year-old boy's finger which she removed ten minutes later. She'd have to tell Dad about it, and she wasn't looking forward to his reaction.

Examining a skater's swollen ankle in his own office, Harry was still thinking about the addict, too. Or, rather, thinking about Rebecca's response to the whole incident. He knew she *would* dwell on it. She'd left him in no doubt of her strong reaction, and he had to admire her for it despite his impatience with her. He was even rather tickled about her attack on his shameless behaviour with Mrs MacInerney.

He couldn't stand the prevailing fashion in certain circles to be blasé and careless about things that really mattered. He knew too many women of his own age and younger whose response to practically everything was a shrug and a laugh and a bored drawl. Like Phoebe Patterson, whom he'd met at tennis and had gone out with for several months recently, the latest in a long line of women whom he'd sincerely wanted to fall in love with but somehow just couldn't. Where was the passion in the women he met? He *liked* passion.

This young skater, Jade, had it.

'When can I skate again?' she demanded, while he still had his fingers on her swollen right ankle.

'Stay off it for four weeks,' he told her. 'You've torn a ligament, I'm afraid.'

'Four *weeks*? But I've got to skate! There's an exhibition at my rink in a couple of months that I have to train for, and I'm going to the Junior Worlds next year!'

'Stay off the ice for four weeks and you'll get there, too,' he told her seriously. 'If you skate on it now, or even in two weeks, you won't. I'll give you some exercises and send you to physio at the health centre, and you should still be able to do most of your off-ice training,' he promised.

'But I'll lose fitness…'

'A bit,' he had to agree. 'Listen, it's not a serious problem, and if you strengthen the ankle off ice it shouldn't recur. Do the same exercises on your good ankle as well, so you won't get the same injury there. This is the foot you land your jumps on, right?'

He touched the bad ankle once more. The foot showed the marks of her stiff leather skating boots in several places. Skaters were like dancers. They suffered for the beauty of what they did.

'Yeah, and I'm working on triples now. Well, *one* triple, and I haven't landed it yet.' She grinned. 'But I will!'

Passion. He responded to it. 'When you come back in four weeks, could you bring me a video of your skating?' he asked Jade. 'I'd like to have a look at what you can do.'

'Really?' She was tickled.

'Sure! I have a few careers I'm keeping track of. A dancer who's aiming for the Australian Ballet. A cyclist who has his eye on the Sydney Olympics. Maybe I'll see you on television in Salt Lake City in 2002 for the Winter Games.'

Twelve-year-old Jade made a dismissive face. 'Two thousand and two? Nah! I'll only be fifteen by then. I'm aiming for 2006…'

Harry threw back his head and laughed. 'That's great, Jade! I bet you make it, too!'

He had his competition track cyclist, Shane McNeill, coming in this afternoon. Shane's pregnant wife Lisa would be here, too, but she would see Dr Gaines. In fact, as Jade Staley collected her mother from the waiting room, the McNeills were already seated there.

For the moment, however, Harry was still more interested in Rebecca. Was it the mobility and sparkle in her face which made it so easy for him to read? At the moment, both those attributes were gone, and her stormy, brooding look was accentuated by that wild, wonderful hair of hers, barely contained in its large tortoiseshell clip. Her sea-blue eyes seemed to emit their own light.

'You're not following doctor's orders,' he murmured to her as they met in the corridor.

'What doctor's orders?' she snapped absently.

'Mine,' he pressed. She wasn't making it easy for him to look after her as Marshall had asked, but he wasn't a man to give up easily. 'I told you not to dwell on it.'

She looked up, startled and suspicious. 'That obvious, is it?'

''Fraid so.'

Letting down her guard a little, she sighed. 'My first mistake here.'

'It won't be your last...'

'Thanks a lot!' The bristle was back, with bells on.

'Don't keep a running tally,' he advised, staying calm.

'Why, you'll do that for me?' The tone was sweet, but he didn't miss the bite behind it.

'Rebecca...' Frustration!

'Harry...' She mimicked his heavy tone, then lifted her chin. 'Your advice is perfectly sound, I admit.'

'Wow! That's a first,' he muttered.

For once she ignored him and finished, 'But you'd be more useful if you could find the little switch in my back marked "obsessing" and click it to the off position.'

'Would it help if I whisked you off to dinner after we finish up?'

'I very much doubt it,' she retorted bluntly.

'Just an idea. No need to snap.'

Harry turned away, and Rebecca could almost have sworn she heard him mutter, 'Why do I bother?'

She bit her lip, knowing she'd been ungracious. Unwise, too, probably. Strategically, it might be better to disguise the fact that she distrusted his motives.

Grace came through at that moment and added to the growing congestion in the waiting-room. 'Lisa?' she said, looking across at Shane McNeill's wife.

The pregnant woman rose, with her husband following close behind her, then stumbled a little just as she reached Grace so that their bellies bumped.

'We'd work very nicely as book-ends, wouldn't we?' the pregnant doctor joked. 'Did you know we're due on the same day, Harry?'

'Christmas, isn't it?'

'Exactly! The twenty-fifth!'

'Makes it look suspiciously unplanned, doesn't it?' Lisa

laughed. 'Who'd choose to have a baby anywhere around Christmas?'

But a frown darkened Grace's features at this. It disappeared so quickly that Harry wasn't sure the McNeills had even seen it, but it made him wonder if Grace's baby was quite the un-clouded blessing everyone assumed. Often, lately, she hadn't looked all that happy...

To deflect attention he told Shane McNeill, 'You're too early, mate. I've got two more patients before you.'

'Not playing the cyclist at the moment, Dr Jones,' he replied cheerfully. 'I'm playing the father-to-be. Lisa says the heart-beat is such a great sound, I've got to hear it for myself.'

'Lisa's right,' Harry agreed. 'OK, then, Shane, I'll be with you later.'

'More room now that those two have gone,' Rebecca said to her next patient, a woman in her thirties who was here for a Pap smear.

Sue Jolly smiled and went through to Rebecca's office. Rebecca was about to follow when Deirdre put her hand over the mouthpiece of the phone and said, 'I've got a new patient on the phone. Or her husband, at least. His name is Dinh Tran and his English isn't very good. He says his wife has a tummy-ache and wants to know if they can come in straight away.'

'A tummy-ache?'

'I know. Not very specific, but I expect he doesn't have the vocabulary for a better description.'

'Well, yes, tell them to come in, then.'

'He also mentioned a baby.'

'A sick baby? Perhaps it's the baby with the stomach ache.'

'Could be. I did have a lot of trouble understanding. Do you want me to try and get it straight?'

'No, don't worry, just tell them to come in and we'll sort it out. Could be anything from indigestion to appendicitis.'

'I'd ring the interpreting service, but I doubt we'd get any-one promptly at this hour.'

'We'll sort it out,' Rebecca repeated, and thought no more about the Trans for the next fifteen minutes until she saw that they'd arrived and were sitting quietly in a corner of the waiting room. Mrs Tran had her head resting rather wanly on her husband's shoulder, and there was no sign of a baby. Could she be pregnant, perhaps? If so, she wasn't that far along because there was no obvious bulge from this perspective.

Was her 'tummy-ache' some kind of gastric upset? It seemed most likely. Surely if there was any real urgency, the Trans would have gone to the hospital's Accident and Emergency department. She saw no need to jump them ahead of the queue.

Shane and Lisa McNeill were standing by the desk, both making follow-up appointments. Lisa needed another prenatal check-up in four weeks, obviously, but Rebecca heard Shane say to Deirdre, 'He wants me back in two weeks to check on the effect of the physio. I can't believe I'm having another problem!'

He looked worried and unhappy. The knee injury must be significant, then. He was lifting his right leg and massaging the muscles around the knee joint as he waited for Deirdre to bring up the correct screen on the computer. His stocky legs looked like hairy tree trunks.

'Mr Radovanovic?' Rebecca called to her next patient.

Half an hour later, at a quarter past six, it was the Trans' turn at last. The waiting-room was almost empty now. They came forward, still quiet and calm, holding hands, and Rebecca saw that Mrs Tran *was* pregnant, though not hugely so. Seated in her office a minute later, Rebecca asked Mrs Tran, 'You've got tummy pains?' as she put her hand across her own stomach, and Mrs Tran nodded.

'Baby,' said her husband, nodding as well.

'Yes, you've got the baby,' Rebecca agreed. 'Now when is that due? About January?'

'No,' Mr Tran frowned. 'Baby is coming now.'

His English might have been elementary, but he'd stated the case with perfect accuracy, Rebecca found when she quickly threw her preconceived ideas about a mild gastric upset out the window and gave her pregnant patient a lightning-fast internal exam.

Mrs Tran was nearly ten centimetres dilated, and if the ambulance managed to get here before the baby did—

Then I'll still need a good, stiff drink! she thought, not exactly panicking but definitely envisaging the possibility of doing so. Had Mrs Tran had any prenatal care? Was she more pregnant than she looked, or was this baby going to be dangerously premature? If so, then they certainly didn't have the facilities for its care here!

'Just stay on the table, Mrs Tran, please!' she told the slightly built young woman as she grabbed the phone.

After ordering the ambulance, she called for Deirdre, who had at least been a registered nurse twenty years ago. Julie Cummings, in her twenties and very well trained, only worked mornings at the moment and had gone home hours ago. Deirdre came, rather faster than usual, alerted by something in Rebecca's tone.

'The panic, probably,' Rebecca muttered, then rapidly listed the equipment she would need if delivery became a reality.

Mrs Tran was still lying quietly on the table, though the contour of her belly had changed even in the ten minutes since she'd come from the waiting-room. The baby was well descended into the birth canal, making an odd, shallow and much softer hollow open up in the formerly drum-hard oval of Mrs Tran's abdomen.

There was no point at this stage in trying to gauge an accurate due date with a measurement of Mrs Tran's abdominal size, and several more questions to Mr Tran failed to get any information. He just didn't understand, poor man, and he was starting to look as alarmed as Rebecca felt. Any minute now…

'Aagh…' A grunt of sheer hard work, rather than a groan of pain.

'Mrs Tran, are you starting to push? Can you try and hold back, please?' Oh, she didn't understand the words! 'Pant. Like this.' Rebecca demonstrated. 'I can hear the ambulance now…'

Mrs Tran panted obediently for fifteen seconds, then shook her head as another contraction intensified and began her hard work once again, just as the ambulance officers, both older, experienced-looking men, came calmly through the door.

Assessing the situation at a glance, one teased, 'You're only just managing to wriggle out of this one, Doctor!'

Rebecca was beyond joking. 'I don't know how far along she is. I told them on the phone. Definitely premature, as far as I can tell. And delivery is imminent. Do you need me to—?' she began, her fists tight.

'Don't worry, we have premmie transport gear in the old bus, and we've delivered a few babies in our time.'

The two men helped Mrs Tran onto a stretcher as she could no longer walk.

'Thank goodness! If I'd had to do it here…'

Mr Tran seized her arm. 'Thank you! Thank you!' He smiled, and even Mrs Tran managed to nod and smile as well. The contraction had eased, but now the next one was already building and she began to strain again.

'Don't thank me… Good luck!'

She just had time to pat both of them on the arm before Mrs Tran was carried off down the corridor. Rebecca followed, trying to keep up, in order to gabble the relevant details of the situation to the ambulance officers as they went. Not that she had many details in her possession! She had no idea, for example, why the Trans had come to this practice. Had Mrs Tran been given any prenatal care at all? Too late to worry about it now. Seconds later, the ambulance had left.

'What was that all about?' Harry wanted to know, handing his last patient file of the day to Bev, the second receptionist on this afternoon.

'I'll tell you over dinner,' Rebecca answered Harry weakly.

CHAPTER FOUR

HARRY took Rebecca to a small Italian place which, she was pleased to conclude, had probably never received the slightest attention from the fashion-conscious. She had no desire to turn this into a big evening. It was early, and it was a quiet night, with just three other groups of diners drifting in during the course of their simple meal.

He orchestrated the situation masterfully, and this—although she'd *never* have admitted it to him—was exactly what Rebecca needed. First, he rang her father and told him where she was. Next, he observed casually that the entrée of garlic prawns and the main course of aubergine lasagne were both excellent. Rebecca dutifully ordered them.

Finally, he told her with a very earnest expression, 'We'll talk about the malpractice suit for three minutes and get it out of the way, then switch to opera or something, shall we?'

'The…malpractice…'

'Gee, you *are* tired, aren't you?'

'Oh. Right. Joke. Sorry.'

'Joke with subtext,' he corrected. 'You didn't do anything wrong, OK?'

'A "tummy-ache"! And Deirdre *told* me his English was bad.'

'Deirdre didn't sense the urgency, and she was the one that spoke to him.'

'But I've dealt with recent immigrants in Melbourne. I should have realised that a young Vietnamese couple with almost no English wouldn't necessarily present the way I'm used to in that sort of situation. The moment I heard the words

51

''tummy-ache'' and ''baby'' from him, I should have put them together, and—'

'Miraculously stopped the pre-term labour?'

'Well, no, but sent them straight to Southshore Hospital.'

'They made it there anyway, right?'

'Just! She was born in the lift.'

'A girl? Nice! They're usually a little stronger than premmie boys.'

'Yes, apparently the baby's looking good, and the mother's textbook-healthy post-partum. She must have been about seven months, judging by the baby's development, although she certainly didn't look it! Dr Gaines—Grace's husband— rang while you were finishing your notes and gave me all the details. He was on hand to deliver the placenta, if not the baby!'

'So what's the problem?'

'They might *not* have made it to the hospital. The baby might *not* have been OK.'

'Do you make a habit of borrowing trouble like that? Let me guess, you're still thinking about that guy who pulled the dislocated shoulder scam, too, aren't you?'

'Of course.'

'Well, unfortunately, you've had your three minutes, so—'

'That wasn't three minutes!'

He looked at his watch. 'True. OK, then, you've got another minute and thirty-eight seconds. What more do you want to say?'

She opened her mouth then stopped and spread her hands. 'I suppose there isn't a lot more *to* say.'

'You've heard the expression ''flogging a dead horse'',' he drawled.

She sighed.

'Right, then, it's on to opera,' he said briskly, rubbing his lightly tanned hands together.

She laughed and took a deep breath, fighting to get beyond

the physical effect he had on her. She *wasn't* going to fall under its spell. It was like a drug, somehow, powerful and frightening. She didn't trust what would happen if she let herself feel this new floodtide of femininity in her body. They had to work together, and Dad didn't need personal tensions between his partners.

'I really appreciate that you've taken the time tonight,' she managed. Good! It sounded firm and sincere, but not too warm. 'I *did* need it. Thanks.'

'Hmm.' His grunted acknowledgment was gruff, brief and noncommittal. And he was frowning. Perhaps *she* appreciated it, but *he* was regretting it? Rebecca wondered uncomfortably. She'd more or less made it impossible for him to get out of it, ambushing him at the end of the day with her change of heart.

Harry *was* regretting it. Her initial rather ungracious refusal had let him off the hook. He couldn't believe it when she'd suggested it again herself just an hour and a half later. He'd filled in the broad brushstrokes of Mrs Tran's drama for himself as everyone had prepared to close the practice for the day, and he understood why Rebecca was feeling dissatisfied. He would have himself in that situation.

And while he was perhaps experienced enough by now to have guessed that something more serious than a gastric upset was going on with the Trans—or at least to have played it very safe and sent them straight to Southshore's emergency department—he didn't condemn Rebecca for her misjudgement.

Far from it. Far, far from it…

She kept doing this to him, and he didn't like it. There was something about her that instinctively drew him, captivated him, set him on fire.

Lust, said a cynical voice inside him. You have the hots for her because she's just the fiery, emotional type you like, especially after Phoebe. Part siren, part white witch—and she even looks the part. Look at her now!

The dark red silk blouse she wore was a little tired after the long day, not crisp any more but soft so that it moulded itself to the very feminine contours of her figure. He couldn't see her matching skirt, but remembered all too vividly the flirting flare of it, swinging around her knees so that even at a sedate walk between surgery and waiting-room today she had looked almost as if she were dancing.

No, it was more than just lust... Oh, God, yes, although he admitted that lust was a huge part of it! It was the passion he'd admired in her earlier. She'd probably go home tonight and unload every detail of today's two very understandable misjudgements onto her father, and Marsh would bend over backwards to assure her that they didn't matter.

Ironically, it was exactly the sort of thing Harry had feared in his qualms about her joining the practice—that she and Marsh would bounce their concerns off each other and thereby double them.

And I ought to be feeling *smug* that I'm turning out to be right, Harry thought as Rebecca murmured to herself, 'I hate to think how Dad will take all this... If it turns out that I'm not up to scratch, he *mustn't* be afraid to let me know...'

Or angry, Harry's thought-track continued, because it really is going to be a damned nuisance. And instead...

Instead, he was intrigued by the way she took things to heart, and ridiculously keen to distract her with scintillating conversation...

Or a searing kiss.

Hell, *no*! The boss's daughter? Since when had he been bent on self-destruction like this?

But she was speaking to him now, the words making her lips part and press together and reshape themselves exactly as they might do under the onslaught of his own mouth—

No!

'You don't seem to have much to say on the subject,' she said, and for about eight seconds he couldn't think of what the hell subject it was. Not her mouth. Definitely not that. Then what? 'Opera,' she prompted.

'Opera...' he echoed blankly.

'Your idea, not mine.'

'Right.' With a huge effort, he redirected his thoughts to a saner area. 'Actually,' he confessed, 'I know almost nothing about opera.'

'Same here.'

'Although I did treat one of the Australian Opera's soloists for a groin injury he sustained during a performance.'

'What made you choose sports medicine?'

'Well, partly because I was frustrated at how little an ordinary GP can do about muscle and joint problems, other than masking them with painkillers, and partly because I'm intrigued by athletes and dancers and what makes them tick— what drives them.'

'And what does?'

'I still don't know. For some, it's simply the will to win. For others, like my skater, Jade, this afternoon, it's almost as if they were born to it. She saw skating on television one day when she was five, apparently, and turned straight to her mother and said, "I want to do that." Till then, she'd been quite a sickly child, I'm told, with a lot of asthma and bronchitis, but as soon as she started skating her health improved and she never looked back.'

'So you believe in the idea of vocation?'

'Absolutely.'

They talked for another hour and a half, and towards the end of it, in the back of his mind, Harry knew he was trying to work out how he could arrange to kiss her... Which was a complete waste of mental effort, as he'd already decided that he wasn't going to do any such thing.

Why, then, did the calculations keep coming?

If I take her arm just outside the restaurant... If I walk her to her car... When she thanks me...

'Thanks, Harry,' Rebecca said. She had signalled for the bill several minutes ago, and here it was, sitting between them on the table in its discreet black vinyl folder, although she wasn't sure that he'd noticed.

Staring down at the dregs of his coffee, he hadn't spoken for at least a minute and neither had she. Fatigue was overtaking her. It had been a long day. She wasn't working tomorrow, though.

'Hmm?' Harry looked up.

'I said thanks.'

'I think you did that already today.'

'Well, I'm doing it again. It was good to get out, and the food was delicious. I'm glad I didn't go straight home. I might not feel compelled to download onto Dad in quite such detail now, especially after your tactful reference to flogging dead horses.'

He grinned crookedly, and she hesitated. The company had been surprisingly pleasant, too. She should probably say that. It would be polite, if nothing else. But she didn't want to.

'Food's always good here,' he was saying. 'And I like the fact that it's so unfashionable.'

'So do I.' It was exactly what she'd noted and liked when they'd arrived.

To illustrate his point, he lifted a Chianti bottle from the centre of the table. Lovingly dusted, it had a half-burnt candle in the top and ripples of sensuously thick white wax running down the curved green sides. It had probably sat on this table for at least twenty years. 'The day they get rid of these...' he said.

'And the red-checked tablecloths?'

'And the red-checked tablecloths,' he agreed, 'is that day I stop coming here.'

She laughed, and got out her credit card. This signalled the start of a polite but deeply serious little tussle over who was paying. He won, but only just and only because he used such grossly unfair tactics—like reminding her she'd spent a very large amount of the bank's money on a new car just last week.

Speaking of cars... They'd parked in opposite directions, as spaces had been scarce.

'I'll walk you down,' he told her, and after the skirmish over the restaurant bill she didn't feel like arguing.

She had her keys in her hand as she reached the vehicle, and was already aiming them at the lock. It must be nearly ten. He must have had quite enough of her company by now...

But then she felt his hand curving lightly and briefly on her hip and turned back to him.

'I haven't thanked *you* yet,' he said, and for one ridiculous moment she was convinced he was about to kiss her.

She froze, her heart pounding. There it was again, that astonishing pull she'd felt between the two of them before— like some effervescent chemical reaction in the air. He was watching her, and his gaze seemed to have trapped hers because all she could do was stare up at him—at his slightly parted lips, his smoky dark eyes and the shadow of new growth which had darkened his jaw perceptibly since this morning.

'I've really enjoyed your company this evening,' he said at last.

'It's been lovely,' she agreed inanely.

Now was the moment, and she knew quite well that she wanted it. It was so obvious. Two people, both unattached. A glass of wine. A palpable, fierce attraction which had built steadily since the moment they'd met.

She didn't think about anything else—forgot about their well-founded flare-ups, her determination to distrust him and her need to prove herself—and could only think of what he would feel like, what he would taste like.

She lifted her face, betraying her need, then heard him sigh between clenched teeth and say, 'You'll be all right to get home? You followed me here from the surgery, but do you know the way back to Centennial Park? You can follow me again, as far as my turn off to Surry Hills, if you like. Just wait for me to get back to my car.'

'There's no need, thanks, Harry,' she managed. 'I have a map. But we're not far west of Anzac Parade, are we?'

'No. Just turn right at the end of the street, and eventually there'll be a T-junction.'

'No problem, then. Night, Harry.'

'Night, Rebecca.'

Unbelievably, she was shaking by the time she sat at the wheel of her car. Would he notice? She looked up to find him already striding away. With his back to her, his big shoulders looked hunched and stiff, and there was something about the rhythm of his walk that made her wonder if he was angry.

She was now. At herself. How had she got it so wrong? And had he guessed?

Of course he had! She'd practically swooned into his arms and puckered her lips!

Was that what he'd been waiting for? she suddenly wondered. Was the whole episode simply a power play for him?

'That's ludicrous, Rebecca Irwin!' she told herself aloud, and drove home.

Dad was still up. The television was on in the small sitting-room, and the ironing-board was out, with the iron standing on it to cool. Several freshly ironed shirts hung on coat hangers hooked to any available spot—the doorhandle, the corner of the mantelpiece.

Dad himself wasn't in sight, but she could hear the vacuum cleaner, droning back and forth in the carpeted hall upstairs. He hadn't heard her come in, and he wouldn't hear her now if she called out to him.

Going through into the kitchen, she found evidence that

he'd had poached eggs on toast for dinner, that he'd mixed up a new batch of muesli and that he'd cleaned out the fridge.

Damn her! Rebecca thought, setting to work automatically to rinse out several containers that held some very dead, very forgotten leftovers. Damn that grasping, two-faced woman!

For six years following Mum's death, Dad had had a very nice elderly housekeeper named Daphne, who'd come in daily, but she'd retired and he'd employed a younger woman in her late thirties, Tanya Smith, on a live-in basis.

Back here from Melbourne for university holidays, Rebecca hadn't particularly taken to Tanya at first, but had kept her opinion to herself. After all, what did she have to go on? Instinct, rather than anything else, and instinct was fallible. She hardly knew the woman. The house had seemed clean and tidy—at least in the obvious places—and the meals had been good. Extravagant, even, at times.

Rebecca had found Tanya in the kitchen one afternoon, eating her way through a whole can of smoked oysters on salted biscuits.

'I have a medical condition where my body doesn't burn food efficiently,' she'd explained glibly. 'I need to snack a lot to keep my weight up. Your dad knows all about it.'

And she'd certainly been thin enough to support the statement. She'd had a certain energy, too, and it had been entertaining to hear her tart, suspicious opinion of politics and world events aired out loud.

Then, after Tanya had been with the Irwins for nearly four years, Dad had flown down to Melbourne one weekend for a visit…and a talk. Over a restaurant dinner, he'd told Rebecca, 'I've come to care for Tanya quite a lot. Of course, it's not what I felt for your mother, but I do care for her. She fits into our household now. She's worked hard for Simon and me. I wanted to let you know what was happening… I'm planning to take her on a cruise and ask her to marry me.'

'Oh, Dad, that's *great*!'

She knew how lonely he had been, Simon's company not-withstanding, and how his loyalty and love for their mother had prevented him, for so long, from falling in love again. Witnessing such grief and coming to understand the depth of love that lay behind it had had a powerful effect on Rebecca.

And at last, ten years after Mum's death, Dad had found a second chance at happiness, albeit of a quieter, less romantic kind.

'Do you know…? I mean, she must already have an idea how you feel.' Rebecca said.

'She must,' he agreed. 'Although I've been a bit old-fashioned about it. I haven't said anything. We're not lovers. But I've given her jewellery and paid for her car repairs. And the cruise ticket, of course. And—if I can say this to my grown-up daughter—the kiss we exchanged on her birthday last week wasn't exactly chaste!'

'I can handle it, Dad,' she told him indulgently.

'So do I have your blessing, Becca?'

'Very much so. And Simon? Is he pleased, too?'

'Simon is…yes, pleased, of course. He's only just out of his teens. I think boys…men…at that age find it very difficult to comprehend that their father could need an emotional life!'

'Well, *I* understand, Dad, and I think it's fabulous!'

So Dad went back to Sydney, and took Tanya on their cruise, and it was a painful, horrible disaster.

He proposed to her on their first night at sea, apparently, and she turned him down. Not kindly, either, but almost an-grily, Dad said, as if she'd been affronted that he, ten years her senior and her employer, could have dared to think of her that way. She dismissed any suggestion that he'd given her fair warning of his intentions, with his gifts and their holiday, and she actually used the words 'sexual harassment', although how a courteously worded proposal of marriage could come under that heading Rebecca had no idea!

With separate cabins, they hardly saw each other for the

rest of the week-long trip, but since their cabins were adjacent, Dad had no trouble discovering that, by the third night of the cruise, she was entertaining the cruise's thirty-two-year-old social director in hers until the early hours of the morning.

When the ship docked again in Sydney, she left with her holiday luggage and he never saw or even heard directly from her again. She actually sent a friend to clear out her room. Needless to say, the jewellery, worth a significant sum in total, was not returned.

Dad phoned Melbourne several times to tell Rebecca the whole story as it unfolded. He was obviously still bewildered at what he saw as his own misreading of Tanya's response to him, and berated himself for not being more sensitive. They had some long, painful talks about it all, and Rebecca twice flew up on weekends, at the expense of her own studies, because she was so concerned.

It took him several months to gain perspective and see that the fault lay with Tanya and not with himself, but even then he was simply not willing to take the same risk again. He hadn't had any help in the house at all for the past two years.

Rebecca washed out the alarming contents of the containers in the sink, put the ironing-board and iron away and gathered up the shirts on their hangers to take them upstairs.

She met Dad in his room, just as he switched off the vacuum cleaner.

'Ah, there you are, gypsy!' he said, taking the armful of shirts and turning to the wardrobe to hang them up.

Rebecca was warmed by the old nickname. He hadn't been calling her Becca lately, which was good, really, because it did sound too childish. She'd always liked 'gypsy', though, and Dad had been so cool and formal with her these past few days that it felt good to hear the warmth in his voice now.

'You didn't have to do all this,' she scolded him, with a dismissive wave at the vacuum cleaner. 'I'm off tomorrow, remember?'

'Well, I didn't intend to do it all,' he confessed. 'But I got into a flow, you know how it is. I was lured on into greater achievements by my own astonishing efficiency.'

'You mean the fridge?'

'Yes, the fridge was a bit ambitious, wasn't it? When I opened that container of potato salad...'

'That's what it was?'

'Er, probably.' He winced. 'I should have realised what I was in for and fled.'

'I rinsed out all the containers and left them to soak in detergent and water overnight.'

'Bless you!'

'Dad, shall I chip in half the cost of a cleaning lady to come in once or twice a week?'

'You know it's not the cost...'

'I know...but is it really still the Tanya thing after all this time? You needn't have anyone to live in. There are agencies these days. It's completely impersonal, if that's what you'd like.'

'Do you think I've been managing so badly?' He smiled.

'No, but in your position...'

'Shall I tell you the truth?'

'Please!'

'It's not Tanya any more, despite the bitter taste that left in my mouth. Before Simon left for Harvard, it had become something we shared and, believe it or not, we both enjoyed it. He'd say to me, ''Time we had a blitz on the house, I reckon, Dad,'' and he'd put on some of his music—which I almost started to like—and we'd go at it.

'Now he's halfway round the world, of course, and you and I probably don't need to achieve parent-child intimacy through house-cleaning, but I've got a bit stubborn. I'm proud of the fact that I do everything here myself, and don't think I'm going to kick back and let *you* do it all now you're here!'

'You're cute, Dad,' she told him tenderly.

'I know.' He smiled smugly. 'But just imagine what a difficult old cuss I'll be by the time I'm ninety!'

'I shudder at the very thought.'

He turned to unplug the vacuum cleaner and wind up the cord, and she noted how fit and trim and youthful he looked at fifty. She had no doubt that he *would* live until ninety and beyond, and remain very much his own man. Illogically, even while admiring his physical and mental capability, she felt a fresh surge of protective love for this unusual and wonderful man.

No one, but *no one*, was going to undermine his certainty about himself, the way Tanya Smith had done! And, after all, she wasn't going to burden him with a long, needy recitation of today's misjudgements over John Morrison, a.k.a. Joe Morrow, and Mrs Tran's early delivery. There was really nothing to be gained by it, and it simply wasn't fair.

The four doctors met for a partners' dinner on Saturday night. Since it was Rebecca's official welcome to the practice, as well as a very necessary opportunity to talk through several practical issues, Grace had suggested the revolving restaurant at the top of Centrepoint Tower.

'Sydneysider that I am,' she said, 'I've never been there!'

So they met there for cocktails at six-thirty, in time to see the sun set behind the city as the view slowly changed to take in the full 360 degrees each hour. Grace stuck to non-alcoholic fruit drinks and Rebecca soon concluded that she should have done the same, since her gin and tonic quickly went to her head—it *had* to be the gin and tonic—and made her aware of Harry again, as she had been so shockingly on Wednesday night.

Staying away from the practice on Thursday had been good, and she'd had a lazy day, punctuated by lunch with an old friend she'd kept in touch with from school. On Friday, she'd gone in to the practice, quite looking forward to seeing Harry for the express purpose of proving to both of them that she could interact with him quite calmly, without the inconvenient interference of either anger or attraction.

Then, of course, she'd discovered he was seeing patients at Hazel Cleary Lodge in the morning, and was taking the rest of the day off! Now here they all were, very nicely dressed—Grace and Rebecca had both chosen flowing, elegant black, while the two men wore dark suits—and prepared to have a pleasant and productive time.

Noting exactly how close Harry's leg was to hers beneath the table as they sat down was definitely not part of the equation! Wine with the four-course meal didn't help, but Dad had already filled her glass to the brim before she could stop him.

And then Harry started talking shop. 'What are we going to do about everyone's hours?' he said briskly. 'I'm a little concerned that these next few months are going to be very messy in that regard.'

'You mean because the patient load isn't building as quickly as we thought it would?' Dad said.

Harry nodded. 'I was talking to the building foreman of the new development yesterday and he said that the next stage won't be finished for another three months. And we didn't get as many people from the low-cost housing in stage one as we thought we might.'

'Southshore Health Centre bulk-bills,' Marshall said. This meant that patients themselves paid nothing for a visit to the doctor. 'I expect that's the reason. A lot of people are choosing the financial savings over the greater continuity and personal contact that we can offer.' The Irwin practice, on the other hand, bulk-billed the government for pensioners and other financially disadvantaged patients, but charged a little more than the basic fee for others. 'That should change with stages two and three,' he went on, 'because those are catering for a different market.'

'You two have been getting some new obstetric patients

from the new development, though, haven't you?' Harry asked Rebecca and Grace.

'Yes, which is great,' the latter said.

'But the fact is, we could still manage to give ourselves each a four-day week, or even three and a half. We just don't have quite enough patients. Julie would like to increase her nursing hours, but I don't think we can offer her that option at the moment. And, of course, in three months when the load does start to build, Grace will be going off on maternity leave.'

'What are you suggesting, Harry?' Grace said.

'Don't know,' he answered cheerfully. 'Some sort of a re-think. I've also been wondering if we should extend our hours on a couple of evenings, and put in Saturday morning hours, too. Most of my patients are at work and some of them have demanding training schedules in their sport or dance. They don't necessarily want to take the time off during the day. Southshore offers evening and weekend hours. I'm wondering if we should do the same.'

'So you're talking about increasing the hours when you've just finished saying that we don't have enough patients for the hours we've got!' Rebecca said, trying to keep her voice calm. Was she simply far too sensitive where Harry Jones was concerned, or was he implying that it was her arrival in the practice which was causing the problem?

'Look, I'm just tabling a few issues that I see as important,' Harry said, with his usual husky rasp of impatience. 'They concern us all equally so I feel we all need to think about them.'

'Have you and Marcus decided how long you want for your maternity leave, Grace?' Marshall asked.

'Not yet.' She looked uncomfortable. 'I'd like to take at least three months, and then only come back part time, but Marcus…seems to feel I'll find that frustrating. He's talking about six weeks, and then returning full time.'

'I think we need a decision fairly soon, if you can, Grace,'

Marshall said, touching her arm. They were seated side by side.

Grace nodded. 'I—I know.'

She looked miserable now, and had hardly touched her food. There was a small silence, then she looked up with a big, bright smile and said, 'Well...!' She obviously hoped that everyone would think she was fine.

Everyone knew she wasn't. As a distraction, Harry topped up Marshall's glass, leaned forward a little and asked him, 'Have you seen Gareth Searle lately? How are things at the health centre?'

Rebecca waited a moment, then asked Grace quietly, 'How are you feeling?'

Grace had been with Dad's practice for close on two years now, and Rebecca liked her enormously. There was only about five years difference in their ages, so they could easily have been sisters, but it was as a mother that Grace would really shine, Rebecca considered.

There was something so warm and giving about her. It was there in her soft, twinkling blue eyes and the rounded fullness of her arms. If there was something wrong with the baby...

'I'm feeling good. Fine,' Grace said brightly. It was a little forced.

'Who does your prenatal care?'

'Oh, I go to Julius Marr at Southshore. It's convenient, and he was at university with my older brother so he feels like a friend. If I develop any sort of a problem, Marcus will send me to a colleague of his, but I've been so disgustingly normal with everything so far...' Distracted from whatever had been upsetting her before, she was clearly telling the truth. 'I'm not exactly stretching Julius's skills!'

So there was nothing wrong with the baby, thank goodness!

'Even Marcus isn't worried?' teased Rebecca. She knew that obstetricians usually *did* worry about their pregnant wives—or their pregnant selves, if they were female—because in their working lives they were always the ones on hand when things went wrong.

'Not worried, no.' The tension was back again.

Rebecca changed the subject quickly. 'Do you have family in Sydney, Grace? I think you do, don't you?'

'Just my mother...' she said slowly.

'Well, that'll be lovely for you—' Rebecca began.

But Grace went on after a tiny pause, 'but I'm afraid we don't speak to each other these days.'

'Oh... Grace, I'm sorry, I didn't know.'

'Why should you? I haven't talked about it, but I don't mind doing so.' She gave a twisted smile. 'Mum didn't approve of my choice of husband, you see, and she expressed her views on the subject very bluntly. More than once! Which wasn't really very useful of her, as we were already married. So I yelled at her, and she yelled at me, and now I think we're both waiting very stubbornly for the other one to pick up the phone first.'

She laughed, then picked up her napkin and wiped away some tears. 'Silly!' she sniffed, smiling and crying at the same time. 'If I'm feeling this bad about it, I shouldn't let pride get in the way, should I?'

'Perhaps not. I know it's hard...' Rebecca squeezed the other woman's hand. So this was the source of Grace's tension!

Out of the corner of her eye she saw Harry glance across, then he spoke to Dad again, as if realising that his best role at the moment was to keep both himself and Dad out of what had become a very female exchange. There, Rebecca had to give him points for sensitivity. Lately, unfortunately, he'd been scoring quite a lot of points that way.

'But Mum was *impossible*!' Grace went on, her round, pretty face darkening again. 'And I just don't think I could *stand* it, at the moment, to hear a reprise of the subject. No, she can make the first move, thanks! She can show me she's not going to harp on about it or say I told you so, and then I'll be more than happy to meet her halfway!'

The waiter arrived with dessert menus at that moment, which reminded everyone that there was still quite a lot to discuss. Grace briskly began to debate the issues at hand. How often were they prepared to talk to each pharmaceutical rep? Twice a year? Or only once? In the case of some of these drug reps, though certainly not all, once was felt to be *quite* enough.

Next, should Harry give up obstetric work altogether? Or did it make sense to have him keep up his skills in that area as a back-up? He'd hardly done any pre- or postnatal check-ups in ages, only stepping in to cover for Grace if she was unavailable at short notice, and he hadn't looked for visiting rights in the maternity ward as he didn't have the special obstetrics diploma which GPs could take to increase their knowledge in this area. Rebecca herself was keen on mothers and babies.

'And I wouldn't want to deny you the chance to build your workload there, when it's really something I'm quite happy not to do,' Harry told her.

The word 'experience' again. At least this time it didn't have the syllable 'in' in front of it! She had to grant that, on this occasion at least, he wasn't aiming a dig at her, but was simply considering her stated preference.

By the end of the evening, though, she couldn't help noticing that every one of the decisions made tonight had gone his way! They'd be introducing evening hours within the next month, and Saturday mornings after Christmas.

Grace looked tired as they all rose to leave. Being only around five feet two, she was carrying her pregnancy rather awkwardly already and it probably hadn't been comfortable for her to sit upright at a table for such a lengthy meal.

The revolving outer ring of the restaurant, where all the tables were situated, was flush with the stationary part of the floor and moved quite slowly past it, but Grace had forgotten about the movement altogether and tripped as she walked towards the lift. Rebecca reached out at once to steady her, and Harry, on Grace's right-hand side, did so, too. Their two hands met in the middle of Grace's back, and as Grace was somewhat shaken and needed the support they stayed like that.

The result was familiar by this time—a melting consciousness of every inch of his skin touching hers, and an instinctive need to seek closer contact. She felt the brush of his olive-green shirt sleeve and heard the familiar scratch in his deep voice as he asked Grace, 'Back on your feet?' Then he teased gently, 'I guess it's difficult when you can't see your own toes.'

'Oh, Harry,' Grace answered indignantly. 'For goodness' sake! I can still see my toes—just!'

His laugh was delectable. And his hand, as it broke contact with Rebecca's arm, left a patch that tingled like the deep-heat rub he recommended to some of his patients.

CHAPTER FIVE

'How's your daughter getting on?' asked Marcus Gaines, meeting up with Marshall in the lift when the latter dropped in to Southshore Hospital on the way to work to see a long-time patient who was recovering from an acute heart attack.

'She's doing well. I'm very pleased,' Marsh said, not willing to go into any detail at a time like this.

He didn't feel he knew Marcus Gaines very well, although they'd met many times, both here at Southshore Hospital and through Grace. The hard-working obstetrician, who had his own private practice and visiting medical officer status at the hospital, was rather reserved. Even this casual query about Rebecca was a bit of a surprise, and if he did have any doubts—for example, that she and Harry weren't as relaxed with each other as he'd hoped—then Marcus wasn't the man he'd choose to confide them to. Grace, in contrast, was so warm and approachable. Perhaps that was why the two of them needed each other.

But what was Marcus saying?

'She almost got caught short and had a premmie infant delivered on her examining table. I ended up finishing the job here after the baby was born in the lift. Touch and go! But, anyway, I'm sure she told you.'

'Er, no! When was this?'

'Just over three weeks ago. She really didn't tell you? I was just going to pass on the news to her that the baby's doing very well indeed now.'

'I'll tell her,' Marshall nodded, while thinking, She didn't breathe a word about it. And neither did anyone else. Why?

Was she scared to tell me? And did she swear everyone else to secrecy? Surely not!

Marcus left the lift at the maternity floor, and Marshall went on up to see his patient in the coronary unit on the eighth floor. Jack Simmonds was doing well, but he was an anxious type and had several questions which he didn't feel the specialists had answered clearly enough. Marshall spent some minutes in reassurance and explanation.

In the corridor on his way out, he encountered another colleague, this time a friend. He'd known Gareth Searle, director of Southshore Health Centre, for nearly fifteen years. They were both heading down in the lift to the doctors' car park so were able to exchange a good bit of news on the way.

'We're thinking of taking on another doctor part time,' Gary said.

'So you *are* getting the increase from the new housing estate?'

'Not as much as we expected, actually.'

'Same here.'

'We expect to need another full-time position eventually, but at this stage...'

They talked about the delayed completion of stages two and three, and how difficult this made it to plan coming needs accurately.

'With Rebecca on hand now, we're all twiddling our thumbs some days!'

'Relatively speaking, of course!'

'Indeed. For someone starting out, though, I'm concerned she's not getting quite enough work and variety.'

Then they looked at each other. Gareth spoke their shared question aloud. 'Would Rebecca be interested in dividing her time between your practice and the health centre?' he asked. 'Until our numbers stabilise?'

'OK, Mr Dunstone, that's all I need to know. If you could make an appointment for next week, I can give you the first round of injections, and we'll have time to complete them all a good two weeks before you fly out. You'll start the anti-malarial treatment about a week before you leave.'

'I've heard some of those vaccinations can really make your arm ache,' said the thirty-one-year-old fisheries research scientist, who was off to Africa for a year as part of an international aid programme.

'They can,' Rebecca agreed. 'For several days. Particularly the cholera and typhoid. You'd better think about which arm you use most, so I can give you the shot in the other one.'

'Hmm. That's not as easy as it sounds.' He frowned. 'I'm right-handed, but I use a computer a lot, which takes both hands, and I tend to lift equipment with my left. Not to mention changing gears, and my job involves a lot of driving at the moment. I'll have to think about it. You don't need to know today, right?'

'No, not until you actually roll up your sleeve,' she told him.

'Ouch!' he winced. 'That's a bit graphic! Hate needles!'

'Worth it, though. And there's one other thing I should stress about Africa. The rate of HIV infection in much of the population there is extremely high over the whole continent, so if you do get involved in any kind of a relationship, please, use a condom.'

'Hadn't thought about that.' The single scientist nodded, looking a little uncomfortable. 'Don't…er…know if it will be relevant, but thanks for the warning.'

To cover the slight awkwardness, Rebecca came in quickly, 'The job sounds interesting, by the way. What exactly will it involve?'

Wanting to put him at ease as she wound up the consultation, and genuinely interested as well, Rebecca was sorry she'd asked several minutes later as his account continued lengthily. It *was* interesting, and the tanned and bearded scientist obviously loved his work, but he was her last appointment of the day and she knew it must be late.

It was! Both Bev and Deirdre, the receptionists who worked on Friday afternoons, had gone by the time Rebecca ushered Geoff Dunstone out and put his file back on the front desk. In fact, everyone had gone. It was well after half past six. Only Harry was in evidence, and he was sitting on the waiting-room couch, thumbing through a magazine as if he had all the time in the world.

'Did you say I could make another appointment now?' Geoff Dunstone asked.

'Well, I did,' Rebecca answered. 'But it turns out it's later than I thought and our office staff have gone.'

She looked at the blank grey screens on the two computers, and knew she wouldn't be able to switch one on again, bring up the correct screen and key in the right details herself. It just wasn't her area. 'Could you phone on Monday? I'm sorry about that.'

'No worries.' He nodded easily, and left.

Harry was just as casual.

'If you want some feedback,' he said, then continued without waiting to give her the opportunity to decline, 'I think you're spending too long with some of your patients.' He closed his magazine and stood up. 'That's why you're running late by lunchtime, and then again at the end of the day. Like now.'

'OK, but I—' she began, but he hadn't finished.

'Of course, I know you want to be thorough—'

'And is that wrong?' she countered defiantly. His patient, pleasant tone was infuriating.

'Of course not,' he soothed, getting her back up still further. 'But I guess you have to be selective about it. If someone comes in and says, "I think I've got bronchitis," and all their symptoms check out but you're concerned about their general health and fitness, too, suggest a follow-up appointment. Don't try and do it all in that first fifteen minutes. You spent thirty-five minutes on Ron Agnew this morning.'

'Gee, you're a walking stopwatch, aren't you?'

He ignored her sarcasm. 'It's good to do that, but you have to schedule it in advance.'

'In the case you're referring to,' she explained crisply, 'I didn't want to give him the chance to wriggle out of it!'

'And why do you think he would have?'

'Dad says he has a history of breaking appointments. And as for just now, it was hardly my fault! I asked a friendly question, and got a much longer answer than I'd expected.'

'OK.' He took a step closer. She lifted her chin and faced him defiantly, just inches away. 'I'm sure there's a reason every time you go five minutes over the allotted appointment span, but the end result, if you do it with half your patients, is that after four hours you're forty minutes late.'

'Yes, Harry, thank you. I think I can work out the maths for myself. You really are intolerable, you know! Intolerable, with your condescending, interfering advice. Robbing me of my confidence and my autonomy. If it wasn't for—'

'Rebecca, you've got it wrong.'

'Oh, really?'

'Yes! I'm trying to help you, damn it! Can't you *see* that?'

His hands gripped her upper arms suddenly. She gasped. His dark eyes were blazing down at her and she could feel the hard press of his thighs against her skirt. For another second or two the anger sizzled between them, then at the same moment they both froze.

His mouth was so close to hers that she could have traced the contours of his lips with her fingers simply by lifting her hand, so close that the heat of their bodies had begun to blend. His gaze raked over her then settled on her mouth. Her lips felt suddenly dry, and unconsciously she let the tip of her tongue slip out in a vain effort to moisten them.

He shuddered, let her go and wheeled around to press his hands on the back of a chrome-framed chair.

'Believe me, Rebecca, I'm only trying to help,' he repeated through gritted teeth.

The doorblind rattled, and here was Dad. He'd been to see Georgina Bennett, he said. Both Harry and Rebecca pretended that nothing was wrong.

'I'll check that we're all locked up,' Harry said at once, letting go of the chair but still not facing them as he started down the corridor. 'You two head off, OK?'

'Right, Harry. See you later,' Dad said easily. 'By the way,' he added a few minutes later as they both drove home in his car together, 'you didn't tell me you'd almost delivered a premature baby in the office, Rebecca.'

She stiffened a little. It was over three weeks since that date, and nearly three weeks since they'd all eaten together at Centrepoint Tower.

'Someone told you, then. Was it Harry?'

She heard the suspicious bite in her tone, but after his attack on her time management just now he was the obvious one to suspect of telling tales out of school, despite what he'd said about helping.

No one had mentioned the subject openly to Dad at the office, which she'd been a little surprised about at first, having expected some teasing or a passing reference. She'd told him briefly herself, the following day, about the man with the dislocated shoulder, managing not to make too much of her own self-doubts.

But perhaps everyone in the practice assumed that she'd thrashed out the subject of Mrs Tran's baby so thoroughly at home with Dad that she and he were both sick of it. Remembering her initial need to unburden herself in detail, Rebecca knew they might easily have been right. She was sure that Harry, however, would not have felt burdened by issues of tact in this case.

Dad seemed surprised at the mention of Harry, however. 'No, it was Marcus Gaines, actually. You don't mind, do you?'

'Well… No, not really.' Not if it was Marcus instead of Harry!

'He wasn't telling tales,' Dad assured her, proving how easy to read she'd just been. 'He just thought you'd like to hear that the baby was doing well. That was this morning when we ran into each other, and I haven't had a chance to pass the message on till now… Well, we've hardly seen each other.'

It was true. Although over the course of the week the work-load in the practice was still a little thin when spread between four doctors, they'd both been busy all day today. This week-end might be busy, too, as Rebecca was covering for Grace, and with two of the latter's pregnant patients already close to or past their due dates, she was fairly confident that she'd be needed.

'It's not the best time for Marcus and me to go away, I know,' Grace had said last week when they'd arranged it. 'But it's the only time he can take before the baby's born, and we really need the break and the chance to spend time together with no pressure and no disruptions. We've booked a bed and breakfast in the Blue Mountains.'

'It should be lovely,' Rebecca had said, and Grace had nodded rather desperately.

'Hope so!'

'The fact that you didn't tell me—' Dad was saying carefully now.

She jumped in. 'I didn't want to bother you, that's all, Dad. I wasn't trying to sweep it under the carpet. She was a new patient. It's not like she was someone you'd already been seeing. But I *was* dwelling on it at first, and I knew I'd probably bore you. Are you angry about it? I will tell you about any mistakes I make in future, if you think it's important for you to know.'

'Take it easy, gypsy,' he soothed. 'I'm not angry. And I

definitely don't want you to feel you can't talk to me—about your mistakes *and* your successes.'

'Haven't had any conspicuous examples of those so far!'

'Saving lives, as we doctors are commonly supposed to do, is often a much less dramatic activity than most people imagine,' he said. 'Didn't I hear Ron Agnew promising you he'd give up smoking just before lunch?'

'Yes, but whether he'll stick to it...' Inwardly she thought, That's one against you, Harry! No quibbles about time management from Dad, if he thinks I've done a patient some long-term good.

They talked casually for the rest of the journey and then, just as they turned off Anzac Parade, Dad said, 'I've asked Harry over tonight.'

'He didn't mention it.' Her casual tone belied her sinking stomach. After their heated scene just now he was the last person she wanted to see.

'I'd have asked Grace, too,' Dad went on, 'only she's away, of course. We'll just get some take-away Chinese, very casual. He can't get here till eight.'

'Well, it's after seven now,' she noted aloud. 'Since there's no food to prepare, I'll just go over the house a bit.'

'Don't go to any trouble.'

'Hardly time to do that in less than an hour!'

Nonetheless, after changing into casual jeans, a cherry-pink T-shirt and matching sandals, she gave the two bathrooms a once-over, swept the stairs, plumped the couch cushions and set the table, then belatedly remembered to put food down for the cat. He usually didn't permit such forgetfulness, dear old thing, although at over eighteen years of age he could scarcely claim to need a high intake of calories!

By this time it was ten to eight so she dashed upstairs to drag a brush through her stubborn cloud of hair and re-apply her lipstick, then decided with the help of her bedroom mirror that the jeans and T-shirt hadn't suffered at all from their encounter with housework. They would do quite nicely. To complete the picture, she had her pager clipped to her pocket. Harry Jones was certainly not going to think that she'd gone to any trouble on his account!

To that end, she made sure she would be very conspicuously doing nothing when he got here, by going out to sit with a book in one of the green wicker chairs on the front veranda. Dad was in the shower.

When Harry arrived a scant five minutes later, however, she couldn't help looking up immediately at the sound of his heavy footsteps striking grittily on the brick path.

He was carrying Gus, and she remembered the first time they'd met, when she'd opened the door to find him there instead of the lazy old pet she'd been expecting. With the animal in his arms, Harry was undoubtedly thinking about that day, too.

She started to say something clever and biting about it, but then he got closer and she saw his face.

'Rebecca…' he began tightly. He wasn't just carrying Gus. He was cradling him.

'Oh, Lord! Oh, Gus!'

'I found him two doors down in someone's front yard,' Harry said.

Coming forward, Rebecca saw the cat's tail flick feebly. 'Oh, he's alive. Oh, I thought he'd been run over!'

'No, but he's very ill, love.'

'Ill?'

'I gave him a bit of a check, and it looks to me like a urinary tract blockage. You could feel it yourself. His bladder's distended and as hard as a stone. Desexed male cats are very prone to it. You probably know that. He's not a happy guy, and he'll definitely need a vet.'

'Can it be relieved?' She couldn't think, didn't stop to wonder why she expected Harry to have all the answers. She was reaching out, stroking Gus's fur, her breathing high and shallow.

'Well, it can,' Harry said. 'He could be catheterised, but it'd have to be under general anaesthesia, and even then the condition will inevitably recur. He'll probably have all sorts of problems from now on.'

'He's over eighteen years old.' Her throat was tight.

'Exactly. I think it would be best if—'

'I meant, we've had him for so long. I—I can't think.'

'You must, Rebecca. It's hard. But you must. He's in pain.'

'What are you saying?'

'I think he should be put down. I think that's the right decision.'

'Just like that?'

'No, not "just like that".'

'And yet you're saying it as if he's an old coat, ready for the charity bin.'

'What I'm saying is that it's unfair to him to agonise about your decision for too long. He's suffering.'

'So am I! Do you think I want to—?'

'Look, Rebecca, once and for all, what is this *about*? You? Or the animal?' His voice was an urgent rasp and his gaze was locked on hers. He was right, of course.

'Gus,' she agreed tightly at last. 'It's about Gus. I'll talk to Dad.'

A dry sob caught in her throat as she reached out for the old cat. He lay so listlessly in Harry's arms that it was hard to hold him properly, although he made no protest at the transfer. She was barely conscious, for once, of the warm, masculine weight of Harry's arms as they briefly shared the heavy, softly furred body.

She was trying to decide on the best course. 'Our vet turns his after-hours calls over to a larger animal hospital. It'll be horrible if there's a long wait. We took him there once before when he'd been in a fight, and they were really busy—cats and dogs everywhere. Gus hated it. Although I suppose he's too ill to care, now... Dad?'

She climbed the steps into the house, and there was Dad at the front door with his wet hair still rumpled from the towel and a question in his face.

Then he saw Gus and his face fell. 'What's happened to the old moggy?'

'I think this is it, Dad,' Rebecca whispered, and quickly repeated what Harry had told her. Her throat was so tight now that the words hurt.

Dad agreed that it would be more cruel than kind to put Gus through anaesthesia and recovery, and a recurrence of the condition in the future.

'Better cancel dinner, Marsh,' Harry said. 'We can drive him over to my father's straight away.'

'Your father?' Rebecca said.

'He's a vet.' It explained how he'd been so quick to understand the problem. 'In Balmain. Not far at this time of night.'

'I'll come,' Dad said, but Rebecca could see that his jaw was working. Although he'd lived in Australia since emigrating from England with his family at the age of seventeen, he still had an Englishman's reserve. He wouldn't want to break down in front of his junior partner and in front of strangers.

'No, Dad,' she told him quietly. 'I'll handle it, OK? It'll be...too hard with two of us. You know what I mean. You...you say goodbye to him. And ring Simon, too. It'll be just after six in the morning there, and he'll want to know.'

Dad nodded but didn't say anything, and Rebecca knew it was because he couldn't.

'I'll get the car,' Harry offered, and went back down the path to melt into the darkness.

Bless him for understanding so easily that Dad wanted this moment alone!

'Do you want to take him?' Rebecca said to her father. 'And

then you can put him on my lap once I'm in the car. I'm going to go in and get his old rug.' The stitched-together squares of mohair that Mum had knitted when he was still a kitten.

Dad nodded again, and took the cat in his arms. 'Byebye, old thing,' Rebecca heard him say as she hurried inside, and when she came out again Dad had his face buried in the soft fur around Gus's neck.

Harry's car was waiting just beyond the gate now, double-parked with the engine idling. Fighting tears harder than ever, Rebecca climbed in and then Dad handed the old puss over. 'Byebye, old thing,' he said again, then turned abruptly towards the house.

It was a very silent drive at first. Rebecca simply couldn't speak, and her thoughts were a repetitive, jumbled mess of imagined and remembered scenes. She thought of Dad on the phone to Simon in Boston, and scraping out the last uneaten meal from a red plastic bowl that wouldn't be needed any more. She remembered how she'd scolded Gus so carelessly when he'd taken her away from eating a meal or watching television with his loud, persistent demands to be let in, and wished she'd made more time lately to scratch his ears and snuggle him on her lap.

'Has this been...?' she began to Harry as they crossed the high span of the new Glebe Island Bridge.

This part of the city could look spectacular at night, with fishing boats moving quietly through the dark water and the Glebe Island container terminal lit up as huge ships unloaded their cargo like stacks of brightly coloured children's blocks, orange and blue and white. Tonight, Rebecca didn't even notice.

'I mean,' she struggled, 'has he been suffering for weeks and we haven't known?'

'I doubt it,' Harry answered. 'My father will tell you for sure. I think there's very little discomfort until the urethra is completely blocked. The past couple of days he's probably been digging in the garden a lot, trying to relieve himself, then trying again. He wouldn't have been able to understand why it wasn't working.'

'Then this morning, or yesterday, I wouldn't have noticed...'

'Ask Dad, but if you're blaming yourself...'

'Oh, of course I am!'

'Don't, love.' His voice was husky. 'He's had a good life for a moggy. And he doesn't know what's happening to him now, beyond the discomfort of that bladder.'

'Mum and Dad chose Gus together and gave him to Simon and me for Christmas when I was nine. Mum loved the black and white ones. "Naughty and jaunty and plain," she called them. "Just what a good cat should be." And Gus had been *so* naughty as a kitten...

'Then, when she was dying—she died at home—and she was getting so weak and thin that she looked like a ghost, she used to have him on her lap for hours, just stroking him...like this. And he'd purr for her. And I'd come in from school to find them both there asleep on the couch, with that transparent white hand of hers still resting on his black fur. Funny. All the good, wonderful memories of my mother, but what I most think of are those last weeks with her at home, dying, and Gus on her lap, purring for her.'

'I'm sorry, Rebecca, I was way too harsh with you just now, forcing you into a decision like that.'

'No, you weren't. You were right. It wasn't fair to Gus. Mum, of all people, would have known that.'

'I was too harsh,' he insisted. 'I hadn't realised how closely he was linked to your mother. I shouldn't have—'

'Oh, Harry.' She gave a helpless laugh. 'Are we going to argue about this, too?'

'I expect so,' he muttered.

'We're not! I—I tend to get on my high horse with you,

Harry. I'm sorry. I don't know why…any more. I'm sorry I overreacted to your advice today, too.'

'Forget it. It's fine,' he growled.

Silence fell again for a moment, while her thoughts ran down old, familiar tracks as she stroked the cat.

'I think my mother's death was the most important thing that's ever happened to me,' she said after a few moments. 'And since Gus was so much a part of it… That's why it's hard to let go.'

'Of course.'

'For Dad, too. He and Mum loved each other so much.'

'You're lucky to have witnessed that.'

'I know.'

'It's how I feel about my parents, too.'

'And I think it's why I haven't got seriously involved with someone yet. Why I haven't just jumped in with both feet. I've seen what real love is, you see, and I don't want to settle for less.'

'Makes sense,' Harry said, huskily and carefully.

He was amazed that Rebecca was saying all this to him, given the bristling hostility she'd directed his way so often. Amazed and moved. He doubted she would be saying it in any other circumstances, but he was treating these moments in his car as a precious gift all the same.

Silence fell again. Rebecca stroked Gus's soft fur gently and scratched and tickled behind his ears and beneath his chin, and when she looked down at him and bent her head lower, she could hear that he was trying, very faintly, to purr for her.

They reached Harry's parents' house in lower Darling Street five minutes later.

The building, made of Sydney's warm-hued sandstone, must once, perhaps over a century ago, have been a commercial establishment—a pub, or perhaps a bakery—but it had been wonderfully converted long since into a professional suite with adjoining residence.

Harry must have rung his parents on his mobile while Rebecca had been inside, getting Gus's rug, because they were waiting together at the open door of the veterinary surgery, which faced diagonally from the corner of the building where busy Darling Street met a quieter side street.

Under the circumstances, greetings were confused and distracted, and Rebecca hardly knew how she got from the car, through the waiting-room and into the surgery, let alone how she managed to absorb several vivid impressions of Dr and Mrs Jones—like a series of still photographs, shot one after the other.

Harry's dark colouring had come from his mother, who was warm-eyed and had long, wavy grey hair caught up in a careless pile on her head. Her hands gave instinctive caresses of support. Harry's father was grey, too, but his skin was much fairer and his eyes were a light golden brown, not glittering black like his son's. There was something comfortable about them both, and as a couple they looked quietly attuned.

'I'm glad you rang, Harry,' Mrs Jones said.

'Let's bring the old fellow through,' said her husband, and he began to examine Gus at once, after taking him carefully from Rebecca's arms. 'Yes, you were right, Harry,' he said after a few moments. 'Not much doubt about what this is. Rebecca, I'm sorry, but if he's eighteen years old I wouldn't recommend putting him through a lot of treatment. Harry said he'd told you it was time to say goodbye.'

She nodded.

'It's an easy death, and it will be especially so today because he's suffering and that'll stop now.' He was preparing a syringe of green-dyed fluid as he spoke. It was a barbiturate drug which would act directly to stop the heart. 'Give him a little pat… See, he's too ill to be afraid, poor old thing.'

'Byebye, Gussy,' she whispered.

'Now…' He quickly clipped some fur from the forearm of Gus's front leg, wet the spot with alcohol and slipped the sharp needle in almost painlessly. Then they all watched silently while Rebecca kept stroking him softly until, within no more than ten seconds, there came a tiny shudder followed by a stillness far deeper than the sick animal's earlier quiescence. Gus was gone.

'Do you want to take him with you?' Dr Jones asked.

Rebecca thought for a moment, tears filling her eyes once again. 'No, I don't think so,' she said at last, shaking her head. 'Dad…said goodbye before. And I think we'd both prefer him to be cremated. Is it just possible to—?'

'We can take care of him, love,' Mrs Jones came in. 'Peter will handle it in the morning. Would you like to come through into the house now? Have some tea?'

'Rebecca?' Harry turned to her with a searching look, then back to his mother. 'Mum, actually, we haven't eaten. I'm thinking…'

'Of course! Eat here! Look, I've got a casserole Dad and I didn't manage half of.'

'That's very nice of you,' Rebecca said, 'Actually, I'd like to. But my father is at home by himself, and—'

'I'll ring him,' Harry said. 'Would that be best? Find out how he's feeling? He may want to be alone. And you do need to eat.'

It *would* be best, Rebecca realised at once, because if she talked to Dad herself she'd really cry, and so might he, and that would be too painful and pointless over the phone. Had Harry really understood so much? She nodded. 'Thanks, Harry.'

She followed him and his mother through to the house, while Dr Jones, senior, stayed behind to finish up in the surgery. Dad had apparently been waiting for a call and, in fact, must have asked Harry to take Rebecca to dinner because she heard Harry say, 'Yes, Marshall, I'll definitely make sure she eats. My mother has something. But how about you? OK, that's good. Yes, OK, we won't hurry home.'

When he'd put down the phone, he reported, 'He's spoken to Simon, he's microwaving some lentil soup from the freezer and he'd rather you didn't hurry home. He wants you to take it easy tonight. That includes dinner so please let my mother feed us. She's a very good cook!'

It was, for some reason, an impossibly beguiling offer. As Dad had said to Harry, there was no sense in hurrying home.

If I did, he'd feel he had to talk, make me feel better... We'd both just make each other feel worse!

Added to that was Harry himself. He'd been so good to-night, and as for his parents... Although her appetite had fled long ago, she could feel the seductively savoury aroma of the chicken and mushroom casserole gradually coaxing it back, and Mrs Jones was already wrapping some large, floury potatoes in paper towelling and popping them into the microwave as Rebecca followed Harry into the big kitchen.

It was a wonderful room, obviously the heart of the house. Warm light bounced off clear-varnished Scandinavian-style wood, and several glass-fronted cabinets revealed a quirky collection of crockery. On a big board, dozens of hooks held a shining array of cooking utensils and there was enough work-top space to gladden any serious cook's heart.

Beyond the kitchen, but part of the same large space, there was an eating area with views through large windows to a night-dark screen of garden greenery and glimpses of rooftops and harbour water beyond. On one wall stood a set of old pigeon-hole shelves, each square hole painted a different jewel-bright colour and each containing a bone china teacup and saucer. No two cups were alike.

'Don't sit at the table yet because it's not ready,' Rhonda Jones said, then firmly refused Rebecca's immediate offer of help. 'Make her put her feet up, Harry, will you?' she added. 'In the armchair by the window.'

Rebecca didn't need persuasion. She was drained now, yet with a sense of peace. She felt as if the atmosphere of this house and its occupants had caught her up and was holding her with as much care as she'd held Gus on her lap in the car.

Sinking into the marshmallow-soft leather of an armchair, she didn't even notice that Harry hadn't joined her until he reappeared beside her and handed her a drink. Gin and tonic. She'd had one three weeks ago at Centrepoint Tower, and he'd remembered her preference. He'd chosen beer for himself.

They drank in silence, while Rhonda hummed snatches of classical music aloud, accompanying the symphony her husband had put on the CD player in the living-room.

Ten minutes later, when their drinks were finished, the meal, including a tossed salad of mixed greens, was on the table.

'I'll leave you to it,' Rhonda said, above the ethereal, floating sounds of a slow movement. 'We've eaten, and I have some phone calls to make.'

'Oh… Harry,' Rebecca said a minute later, once they were alone, using her arm in the air to finish the sentence.

'OK?' he asked, throwing her a searching glance.

'I…' But it was no good. She just couldn't find any words.

He seemed to understand. 'Don't talk, then.' He smiled.

So they ate in silence, and it didn't feel awkward at all, just soothing and warming and right.

Finally, at the end of the meal when Rhonda came back to see how they were doing, Rebecca found her fluency again. 'Thank you so much for this, Mrs—'

'Rhonda, love, please!'

'Rhonda, then. It's delicious, and I feel so much better.'

'You've had an emotional evening. There's dessert, too, if you want it.'

'Oh, I couldn't. I—'

'Like to go for a walk, then?' Harry said lazily.

'Yes, go on. It's a lovely night. And walking at night…well, it helps, doesn't it? No!' Rhonda lifted a hand. '*Don't* offer to clean up! Harry doesn't bring me friends of his who need looking after nearly often enough these days!'

'You mean he used to?' Rebecca couldn't help asking.

Rhonda laughed. 'Daily, my dear. *Daily!* Frogs, lizards, even a rat with a broken leg once. I'd never realised the Balmain peninsula had so much wildlife.'

'I thought you meant people…'

'People, too, every now and then. Once an old homeless man who'd had a mild stroke down by the ferry wharf. And a runaway little boy. "He can live here with us, can't he, Mum? He says he hasn't eaten since *yesterday*!" You were eleven, I think, Harry.'

'Eleven? OK, stop there, Mum, please, because I hate to think what you'd come up with if you reminisced any further back into my colourful past!'

Rebecca was laughing. Somehow, the image of Harry as an eleven-year-old rescuer of lost and frail souls, both human and animal, was a very vivid one.

Outside, there was a cool night wind blowing. It was fresh and delicious, but chilly still at this time of year. Wearing a lightweight pale grey sweatshirt himself, Harry noticed her short sleeves and her immediate shiver and went over to his car.

From the back seat he pulled a jacket of soft brown leather, saying, 'Here, I don't need it.' She plunged her hands down the long satin-cool sleeves and shrugged it up onto her shoulders.

The thing was way too big. The cuffs came below her knuckles, the collar brushed the tops of her ears and the gathered waistband, designed to sit just above his hips, reached down to her thighs. It was heavy, too. Heavy and enveloping and subtly giving off his unique scent. As she had in his parents' house, she felt cocooned, safe, warm…and intensely drawn to him.

'Let's go,' he said.

They walked in the aimless, exploratory loops and zigzags and backtracks that Balmain's old, narrow streets allowed. It was a fashionable and very expensive part of Sydney now, but once, and only a generation or two ago, it had been largely a dockworkers' suburb, and so tough that a long-time premier of New South Wales had been able to boast backhandedly of his own childhood there that, 'Balmain boys don't cry.'

The famous phrase scarcely applied any more. Now the old workers' cottages had been expensively renovated and extended, and the shops and restaurants along Darling Street were quintessentially trendy. Still, with working wharves and back yards still visible from many places, and the streets hilly and crowded, something of the old character of the place would always remain.

'Your parents must have been here for a while,' Rebecca hazarded.

'Since 1961,' he confirmed. 'I was born at the local hospital.'

'Then you're a "Balmain boy", too.'

'You're thinking of Premier Wran. But by the time I came along there was no need for a Balmain childhood to be rough. Mine wasn't. But my parents didn't exactly have a cushy practice then. Pet owners round here often weren't reliable in paying their bills. Things only became comfortable for them in the early eighties.'

'Why did they choose Balmain?'

'They loved the atmosphere. The harbour, the ferries, the wharves. And not just the pretty parts of the harbour, like you get on the North Shore or in Vaucluse and Rose Bay. They loved being at the working end of it, and so did I.'

'From what your mother said tonight about the "friends" you brought home, I'm surprised you didn't follow your father's career path.'

'You're not the first person to say that.'

'I didn't think I would be,' she retorted lightly. 'It's not a very original observation. I just happen to want to know the answer. Why didn't you?'

'Aha. Putting me on the spot. If you want the truth, a big part of it was that I just didn't think I'd be able to compete. Nor did I think then, at eighteen, that I'd be able to stand working with the old man, although I'd done it a lot in the holidays as a child.'

'Not stand working with him? Really?'

'I was a teenager, remember? So I chose medicine, where I could succeed in my own terms, without either of us having to measure ourselves against the other. It was the right decision, too. I love what I do.'

'Was he disappointed?'

'No, he's far too sensible for that. He's interested in what I do, though, particularly the sports side. And the feeling is mutual. We expand each other's horizons. Mustn't leave Mum out of it either. She has a good, active brain. She was his practice nurse and receptionist for years. Now she's enjoying a well-earned retirement, dotes on my sister's two girls—they live about an hour away, up near the northern beaches—and gardens, cooks, and potters— No, that's not right.'

'Potters around?'

'No, pots. Does ceramics. Is a potter. You should be able to say it, shouldn't you? "She paints" after all. But "She pots"? "She potters"? Doesn't work. Logic-less language we have!'

They walked and talked, talked and leaned on the railing at the Darling Street ferry wharf, watching the full moon, walked in silence, talked some more, decided at least three times to strike off down another street rather than head back, until finally Rebecca said with great reluctance, 'You must take me home, Harry. Dad will be wondering what's happened to me.'

'Yes,' he agreed. 'Yes, of course, he will.'

And suddenly, what had been safe and nourishing and right *wasn't* any more. It was utterly dangerous. The emotions of the evening had left her vulnerable and without the strength to fight what she knew had been building between them for four weeks, inextricably mixed with their hostility, and when she made the mistake of looking into his face...

They came towards each other slowly. 'Rebecca...' Her name was a frustrated, impatient rasp, so low it was almost a whisper. His dark eyes had the depth and fire of jewels. They both knew that a kiss was just seconds away, inches away, but he was still holding back, as if pretending to himself that he still possessed the luxury of being able to change his mind.

They both knew he didn't. Rebecca didn't either. She waited, strangely content to let him make all the moves, though her short, shallow breathing, parted lips and raised jaw left him in no doubt as to what her response would be.

'This jacket's much too big for you,' he murmured, studying the garment with a frown as if they might yet get deflected by the absorbing interest of this issue.

'I love it that way,' she answered.

Then he took her shoulders and pulled her towards him as he smoothed back the soft leather collar and slid his hands in a whisper-light caress along her neck and back into her hair. Now, a moment later, he was holding her upper arms and his mouth was an inch from hers. She couldn't breathe...

At last their lips met and clung and moved together, soft and warm and perfectly attuned. She'd had no idea a kiss could generate such chemistry, and had never felt such strength and sureness in a man's body. All those clumsy pursuits in her teens and early twenties, the one man she'd almost slept with—nothing had prepared her for the overwhelming force of her response to Harrison Jones.

She felt as if someone had taken a great wooden spoon and stirred up the bubbling cauldron of her insides like a witches' brew, and the melting sensation that started at her swollen mouth overflowed and ran down through her centre, then pooled in the female core of her body at the meeting of her thighs.

'Oh, Rebecca, I want you so badly,' Harry rasped, and she

could hear that the words were torn from him reluctantly…almost angrily.

She dismissed any thought that his tone was a warning. After all, in many ways *she* was reluctant about this, too, after the angry sparks that had flared between them before tonight…

In fact, tonight was the first time there *hadn't* been sparks of that kind. He had been so good and so perfectly attuned to what she needed. She felt that their knowledge of each other had deepened immeasurably in the space of hours.

Wrapping her arms around his neck, she said against his lips, 'Thank you, Harry. Thank you for tonight.'

'We'd better get back,' he answered gruffly, then came back three times for more as they each tried to tear their swollen, tingling mouths apart.

Finally, with hands held so that their fingers were tangled together, they wandered back to his parents' house, each too reluctant to speak lest they break this strangely perfect end to the evening.

CHAPTER SIX

'IDIOT!' Harry chastised himself in the car forty minutes later as he drove away from Centennial Park and back to his own house, a modest but attractive terrace in Surry Hills. 'Damned great idiot!'

And yet, looking back on the evening, he didn't see how he could possibly have escaped kissing Rebecca as he had. From the moment he'd found the old black and white cat lying on the steps of a neighbour's front path, too much had been stripped away. He'd had no protection left against the clamouring demands of his male response to her.

Even so, the strength of what he'd felt as he'd held her in his arms and joined with her in that aching, endless kiss had taken him by surprise. He'd known all along that he was attracted to her, beyond the angry fire that generated so many sparks. He had felt the feeling grow steadily, but the surge of raging, triumphant desire that the touch of her mouth had released in him had been stunning, shocking...and impossible.

How he'd restrained himself from kissing her again outside her father's house just now, he didn't know. And what he was going to do about the whole thing from now on didn't bear thinking about.

Didn't *require* thinking about, really. He knew quite well that he couldn't allow tonight's passionate release to repeat itself. She was Dr Irwin's daughter, and he was still far from convinced that it was in her own best interests, or that of the practice as a whole, to have her working there.

They hadn't touched on that issue at all tonight, but if Gus's fatal illness hadn't intervened they would have done because Marshall had something to say about it, and he was fairly certain that in those circumstances he and Rebecca would have ended up in the middle of another blazing row instead of the kiss of the century.

Rebecca herself didn't know that, of course. Marshall himself had hinted quite plainly that she didn't know there was any practice business on the agenda for this evening.

I must ring Marsh tomorrow and find out what he was going to propose. Hopefully he'll have talked it over with Rebecca herself by then. We need to get this resolved, he thought as he turned into the narrow rear lane that led to the garage behind his house. *I need to get it resolved,* he amended more decisively a moment later. Because, for the first time in his life, he *wanted* something without being sure that he was prepared to take the risk of going for it.

Rebecca couldn't sleep. She wasn't surprised. Who could, after a kiss like that? After an *evening* like that!

She and Dad had exchanged a long, silent hug in the hall. Neither had wanted to talk about Gus just now, but the silence had left Rebecca with plenty of opportunity to wonder if it was at all possible for Dad to smell Harry's aftershave, clinging to her skin.

She'd shed his jacket in the car with aching reluctance, and not just because the night had cooled off markedly. No, she'd wanted to keep the jacket—wear it all night—because the sense it gave her of him surrounding her, of his scent and his warmth and his maleness, was so wonderful. She'd *never* felt this way about a man's body!

'Not cold, gypsy?' That was all Dad had said to her.

'Harry lent me his jacket.' It felt delicious just to say it.

Dad had been on his way up to bed and she didn't delay him, just assured him, 'I feel a lot better now. Harry's parents were wonderful.'

'I'm glad...'

'But I'm not sleepy yet. Think I'll have some hot chocolate and read a book.'

She'd done that for over an hour, and knew it was horribly late. Still sleep wouldn't come. In bed, with the light off, she relived the touch of Harry's mouth over and over again, relived the broad press of his chest against her breasts and the hard warm weave of his arm muscles as he'd held her, the scent of him, the taste of him, the sound of his quickened breathing.

At that moment, giddy and drained and aching, anything seemed possible—anything, as long as it led to more of those heady, melting moments in his arms. Their past hostility seemed foolish, and the future—seeing him, being with him— tasted sweet with promise.

When she did finally fall asleep at almost two, she had a smile on her lips.

A rude awakening came two hours later. Her pager went off. One of Grace's patients was ready to have her baby. She groped for the phone and rang her after-hours answering service to get the number, thinking groggily, If it's Mrs O'Donaghue, it's her first and I can probably go home to sleep, but if it's Mrs Mikulic...

It was Mrs Mikulic, and she was expecting her third. 'Seems to be hotting up pretty fast, Dr Irwin,' she said, sounding a little panicky. 'Michael timed the last two contractions at less than two minutes apart, and it...uh-h...feels pretty...uh-h...intense.' She began to pant.

'Go to the hospital, Mrs Mikulic,' Rebecca said, feeling herself swim up into greater alertness. She wouldn't be getting back to sleep for a while. 'Get yourself checked in and I'll meet you there as soon as I can.'

She grabbed a quick shower, hoping it wouldn't wake Dad. She needed it, though, to give her a jolt of energy. Then she scribbled him a quick note in case this took longer than expected, and left it on the kitchen table.

Southshore Hospital was quiet—except for the maternity department, which seemed to be firing on all cylinders. There were at least eight women in active labour, and even as Rebecca hurried down the corridor towards Mr and Mrs Mikulic in room five she heard the oddly mechanical cry of a newborn from one of the delivery rooms.

'Dr Irwin?' a thickly moustached man of about thirty demanded anxiously of her as she breasted the doorway.

'Yes.' She held out her hand. 'Sorry, we haven't met before.' She turned to her patient. 'But Dr Gaines has told me all about your history, Mrs Mikulic, and that the baby's going to be a boy.'

'Again!' The mother smiled wryly.

'You were hoping for a girl this time…'

'Well, we *were*,' Mr Mikulic answered for his wife, 'but, really, as long as he's healthy… Three boys will be great.'

The baby *was* healthy, and didn't keep them in suspense for long on the issue. Helen Mikulic reached full dilation just fifteen minutes after Rebecca first examined her, although she had to push heroically then. A hard-working twenty minutes of it brought the head safely out. Another push and the shoulders turned easily, and moments later the whole slippery, purple little body was safely in Rebecca's hands.

Soon afterwards, with the drama over, bed and a late sleep-in began to beckon.

No such luck. A call from the answer service conveyed the fact that Grace's other patient was in labour now as well. Alison O'Donaghue was expecting her first, and had been in slow early labour since about lunchtime the previous day. Now, at last, the pains were only five minutes apart, and Rebecca could tell over the phone that Alison was keen to come in. She sounded tired and discouraged already at how slowly things were progressing.

'Will it all get going now?' she wanted to know on the

phone. 'I'll have the baby by lunchtime, won't I? I mean, that'll be twenty-four hours…'

'We'll see how it's coming along.' That was all Rebecca could promise.

The O'Donaghues lived a good ten minutes' drive from the hospital so she went to the ward kitchen for a coffee to pick her energy up, and there was Dad's old friend Gareth Searle on the same errand.

'Are you between babies or between contractions, Rebecca?' he teased, filling his cup from the bubbling stainless-steel urn.

'Between babies. How about you?'

'Just one baby for _me_. So far at least. Looks like a busy night here. But mine's in active labour and eight centimetres dilated at last count so I'll be needed pretty soon. By the way, I'm very pleased to hear that you're coming to work for us.'

'I'm…sorry?' Rebecca said blankly.

'At least…' He'd seen her face. 'Sorry, I guess it's not quite a done deal. You'll want to have a talk with us about hours, take a look at our set-up, but Marshall seemed to think you'd have no problems with the idea. Was he wrong?'

Instinctively, she closed ranks with her father. 'No. No, of course he wasn't. It's… It's… But, as you say, it's not quite a done deal.'

'Dr Searle?' said a nurse in the doorway.

He took a gulp of his coffee, then poured the rest down the sink as he said, 'Looks like I'm required. Anyway, look forward to talking to you soon.'

Alone in the kitchen, Rebecca's head was whirling and her cheeks were on fire. Gareth Searle thought she was coming to work for him? At Southshore Health Centre? And he'd obviously been talking to Dad.

Taken by surprise, she felt instantly betrayed. Just what kind of horse-trading had been going on behind her back? Was this Dad's idea? She very much doubted it! _Harry_ was the one who didn't believe she fitted into the practice. At some level, she was quite positive this came from him.

If it hadn't been for last night, she might have been able to deal with the thing fairly calmly and sensibly. After all, she'd known from day one what Harry's qualms were. He'd been honest about them—*then*. But the way he'd kissed her, listened to her, understood her, jarred brutally against what Gareth Searle had just told her.

To think he could have been…*seemed*…so wonderful last night when all along, underneath, he'd known about *this*…

She could only see it as a manoeuvre to oust her.

Downing her coffee without even tasting it, she was ready for the O'Donaghues when they arrived some minutes later.

'I don't like this,' Mrs O'Donaghue whimpered, slumped in the wheelchair that had brought her up from the accident and emergency entrance. Then she joked feebly, 'Can't I come back and do it tomorrow?'

Rebecca left the couple alone while Mrs O'Donaghue put on a gown, then came back to examine her, hoping for the patient's sake that she'd have some good news. Unfortunately, she didn't. The baby's heartbeat was strong and steady, but after nearly eighteen hours of mild but steady labour Mrs O'Donaghue was still only one centimetre dilated. She had a very long way to go, and the baby was also presenting 'sunny side up'—in other words, with the back of its head against Mrs O'Donaghue's spine, a position which could markedly increase her discomfort.

'Things do seem to be going quite slowly. If you'd like to go home again, you can, Mrs O'Donaghue,' she offered.

The suggestion wasn't well received. 'Home? Oh, please, no! That'd be like starting all over again.'

'That's fine, then, if you want to stay in. How about walking for a while around the corridors? That often helps speed things up.'

'But I'm so tired already…'

'How about having a lie-down for a while, darling?' Graham O'Donaghue said anxiously, 'and then we'll try the walking?'

'OK.' She nodded with a watery smile.

Rebecca went to check on Michael Mikulic junior in the nursery—doing beautifully—then headed home, suspecting it would be some hours before she was needed back at the hospital again. It was only just dawn, and Dad was still asleep. Gratefully, she folded herself back into bed, and was by now so tired that she conked out at once and stayed that way for several hours, deeply asleep. Awaking to a late breakfast, she found that Dad had gone out, which left her frustrated as she couldn't forget Gareth Searle's cheerful words about 'coming to work for us'.

Picking up the phone, she rang Harry, but there was no answer. Perhaps that was for the best because she knew what she'd have said to him!

Now, though, the angry words gathered inside her, making a painful knot. She spent a restless day. Dad didn't come back, and she remembered now that he'd been invited to a wedding in Newcastle, over two hours' drive away. In fact, looking at the note she'd left for him, she now found added to it, alongside a tiny sketch of wedding bells, 'See you whenever!'

Meanwhile, the hospital could phone at any time with news of Mrs O'Donaghue, and there seemed no point in embarking on something—a walk through the park, say, or some shopping—which she'd then have to abandon at a moment's notice.

The hospital didn't phone, though, and finally she rang the labour ward herself, to hear from midwife Denise Clews, 'We were just about to ring you. She's had a long day, steady contractions at about three to five minutes apart and intense enough that she can't get comfortable, but she's still only three centimetres and her waters haven't broken yet. She hasn't wanted pain relief so far, but now she's getting very discouraged. We popped her on a monitor, but there was no sign of distress from the baby. Do you want to come in and talk about options with her?'

'Yes, I'll be right there.'

'I'm just exhausted, that's all,' Mrs O'Donaghue said tearfully, after another examination showed a gain of half a centimetre's dilatation in the past hour. 'I haven't slept in thirty-six hours—and I had a bad night then anyway. And now I'm getting nowhere! Not even near halfway.'

'I know.' Rebecca nodded.

'No, you don't!' Alison stormed.

'OK. I'm sorry. I can *imagine*,' Rebecca soothed in reply. 'Let's talk about options. You could have some mild pain relief and try to get some rest, but that might slow things down even more. Or we could give you a synthetic hormone to try and speed things up. There's also epidural anaesthesia, which again might slow you down but would give you very thorough pain relief. You could perhaps even sleep.'

'I didn't want any of that. I was so determined! But now it sounds good. Maybe I'll go for the epidural.'

'First, though, I'm going to rupture your membrane because that can speed things up, too.'

She took a special hook and barely had to brush the membrane with it in order to release a gush of fluid—fluid which should have been clear and pale but instead, on this occasion, was stained a dark, ugly green. Denise saw it at once, and they exchanged a look.

Graham O'Donaghue was watching as well. 'Is that…what it's supposed to look like?' he said.

'Not quite,' said Rebecca. 'It means the baby's had a bowel movement in the uterus, which is usually a sign of distress.'

'Distress? What does that mean?' Alison O'Donaghue suddenly forgot about her pain and fatigue.

'It's all right. The monitor shows that the heart rate is still good, but it means we'll have to hurry the baby up a bit. I'm afraid you may need a Caesarean.'

Mrs O'Donaghue took the news well. In fact, she almost seemed pleased because it put a limit on the process—and the pain.

'Is there anyone in particular you'd like to call for a Caesar?' Denise said to Rebecca quietly.

'No, just whoever's available. I'd rather not do it myself. The head's well down and it's a big baby. It might be tricky.'

'I think Marcus Gaines is already here. He's just finished another Caesar in theatre one.'

'Marcus Gaines?' Rebecca echoed blankly. He and Grace were supposed to be away. Denise must have made a mistake.

She hadn't, though.

Another check on the foetal monitor a few minutes later showed that the O'Donaghue baby's heart rate was beginning to dip markedly with each contraction so there was no question now that a Caesarean was the safest route to take, and under general anaesthesia to speed things up. Caesareans were possible, and done frequently, under epidural. It was great for the mother to be conscious and alert at the birth, but this form of anaesthesia took longer to administer and to take effect.

Accordingly, the anaesthetist was called and Mrs O'Donaghue was quickly wheeled to theatre two to prepare her for surgery, with her anxious husband now relegated to the corridor where he could see something of what was going on through the windows.

Rebecca and Denise both prepared to assist, and just as the patient was ready Marcus Gaines did indeed sweep through the doors as if impatient to begin. He was clearly in a black mood, and Rebecca concluded it was fortunate that Mrs O'Donaghue *was* under general anaesthesia. The atmosphere in theatre two was not pleasant.

'Why did you wait so long?' he demanded of Rebecca as he began the incision, then waved away her attempt to reply.

She swallowed her anger. They *hadn't* waited! The monitor had shown no signs of distress at first, and many first labours went longer than this with no complications. It was only the staining of the waters which had signalled a potential problem, and then had come the tell-tale dropping of the foetal heart rate.

Was he always this unfair? She'd only met him once or twice.

And why, for heaven's sake, was he *here* when he was supposed to be in Katoomba, having a romantic weekend with Grace?

'It's a girl,' he announced a few minutes later. 'Looking good...'

'No sign that she's inhaled any of the meconium,' Rebecca said after a few more moments. The baby's breathing was clear and without effort, and there was no sound of congestion in the lungs.

Rebecca and a nurse had suctioned out the baby's nose and mouth with extreme care, and wiped her little face well before giving her any encouragement to breathe. Meconium in the lungs could be dangerous, and even fatal, in a newborn, clogging the delicate folds of lung tissue and leading to a type of pneumonia. The danger would not be fully past until the baby was a few days old, when they'd safely be able to conclude that nothing had been breathed in.

Dr Gaines had already delivered the placenta and was preparing to stitch the incision, against the backdrop of healthy newborn cries and businesslike action from the rest of the team.

Rebecca was soon able to take the baby over to the window, where Graham O'Donaghue looked in helplessly. She gave him the thumbs-up sign. He grinned back and nodded, intensely relieved. In a few minutes he'd get his first chance to hold his new daughter, while his wife was still under anaesthesia.

Marcus still wore a black expression as he worked with his intricate suturing, but everyone else had relaxed a little now that the baby was looking so good. Under cover of two nurses conversing, Rebecca asked him, 'Weren't you and Grace supposed to be away? I'm covering for her. That's why I'm here.'

Marcus looked very much as if he wished she hadn't asked, but she didn't care.

'We came back,' he said abruptly. 'It…wasn't working out.' There was a tiny pause. 'The place we were staying at was horrible. Grace is at home. I rang about a patient I was particularly concerned with and was just in time to come in and deliver her by Caesarean. Does that explain things?'

'Yes, I was just concerned about Grace, that's all.'

Again there was a beat of silence, then Marcus said, 'Grace is fine.'

She's not. I know she's not, Rebecca thought. But he's made it quite clear he thinks it's none of my business. I don't believe their bed-and-breakfast was 'horrible'. Grace was so looking forward to it! But I guess it *is* none of my business so there's nothing I can do…

That argument did not, however, apply to what Gareth Searle had said this morning. That *was* her business, and she'd been able to do nothing about it all day. The fact was knotted even more tightly inside her now because of this new concern over Marcus and Grace.

It was just after seven when she left the hospital, having stayed around to give a full report to Graham O'Donaghue on his precious new daughter, and she knew Dad wouldn't be home yet. She also knew where Harry Jones lived.

Too wound up to consider the wisdom of the action—it had, after all, been a very long, very emotional and very exhausting twenty-four hours—she roared up Anzac Parade from the hospital and turned off into the maze of Surry Hills streets that led to his house, fully prepared to do battle.

He was home, but evidently hadn't been for long because he greeted her at the door dressed only in jeans.

Only in jeans. The droplets of water gathering on his shoulders from his shower-wet hair didn't even count as accessories, let alone as adequate covering for that impossibly broad and masculine chest. It hardly helped her mood that she was immediately mesmerised by the silky thatch of black hair that spread between his dark brown nipples.

And even his humour got her back up tonight. 'I guess we're even now.' He grinned. 'Although I'd argue that my jeans give away a bit less than your towel did that time. Hi…'

She ignored the caress in that last word and refused to spend any time on small talk. 'What's going on, Harry?' she demanded.

'Uh… You tell me. I've just got back from tennis and I've had a shower. Come in.'

She turned to glare at the street behind her. It was crowded with parked cars on both sides, and there were several people coming and going. Yes, all right, of course, she had to come in. She could scarcely have a shouting match with him here on his front doorstep.

He led the way down a narrow front hall, half-filled by the stairs that climbed to the upper floor, and she was too impatient for the truth to take any time observing the place. She got a vague impression of art on the walls and a clean, light colour scheme in paint and furnishings against polished golden floorboards, before reaching his kitchen and fielding his offer of a drink.

'No, thanks. I won't be here long.'

'Oh. Right. Well, in that case, you won't mind if I have one,' Harry said mildly, pulling a beer from the fridge.

His pulse had leapt at the sight of Rebecca on his front step, though he'd hidden the fact well. He'd needed to! He'd decided quite categorically last night that his attraction to

Rebecca Irwin was going nowhere—or, rather, that he couldn't possibly take the risk of letting it go somewhere.

He'd also decided—and this already seemed foolish—that nipping the feeling in the bud ought not to be that difficult if he was really firm about it. He was a man, after all. Men were classically able to divorce lust from any other aspect of their lives…weren't they?

Perhaps not. He'd felt the most absurd exultation on seeing her at the door, and the fact that she looked tired and somewhat wilted in her soft black pants and cream knit blouse didn't do a thing to lessen the feeling. In fact, it only added an unsettling thread of concern to the lethal mix inside him. She'd had a bad night. A bad day. Her hair was a glorious messy tangle of dark colour. She'd come to him again for what she'd needed from him last night—caring and support—and he ached to give it to her, with the touch of his hands and lips against every inch of her.

Now, though, he knew that she was angry, and he should view the distancing effect of this emotion with relief.

But I don't. God, I want her… What the hell am I going to do?

'I ran into Gareth Searle at the hospital this morning,' Rebecca began, and waited for a damning reaction. There wasn't one.

His face was bland as he took a gulp of his beer. 'Oh, yes?' Not that she trusted this apparently innocent reaction!

'He told me,' she pressed on angrily, 'that he was pleased I was coming to work with them at Southshore!'

'I don't understand,' Harry responded blankly.

'Neither do I!' she flared.

'I knew they were interested in someone part time and flexible while we all work through this difficult period with the new housing development. Look, have you talked to your father today?'

'No, I haven't seen him.'

'I tried to ring him this morning—'

'Why?'

'Because I knew he had something to talk about last night. A proposition to put. I thought he'd have discussed it with you over breakfast, since we missed out on dinner together last night.'

'I expect he would have,' Rebecca answered, 'but I got called out at four and then slept in, and he had to drive to Newcastle for a wedding and pick up a gift on the way.'

'I wonder if Gareth and your father talked about you splitting your time between Southshore and us,' he said slowly, then took another long pull on his beer.

'Are you really trying to tell me,' she demanded bluntly, 'that this *isn't* your doing? That you haven't been using Gareth Searle and Southshore to manoeuvre me out of the practice?'

'*Manoeuvre* you?' He set his beer can down on the kitchen bench with a rebellious thump. 'Rebecca, the word ''manoeuvre'' isn't in the dictionary when it comes to me, and you'd better understand that right now. If I wanted you out of the practice, believe me, there'd be no ''manoeuvring''. You'd know up front that I was unhappy about you, and why, and so would your father. Grace, too, for that matter. I think you dividing your time between the two practices would be a great move all round, but not because I've got anything to complain of in the way you've worked so far.'

'Yet at the beginning—'

'You knew what I thought at the beginning, and I stand by that. Experience elsewhere would be good for you—and for your father. There have been some awkward moments. But nothing that would cause me to manoeuvre you—or even firmly nudge you with the toe of a big boot—out of the practice.'

'Right. I see,' she answered lamely. No one could argue with that degree of energetic indignation and not mean what they said!

He was smiling now. 'That flappy look suits you, by the way,' he said.

'Flappy?'

'When the wind's just been taken out of your sails.'

'Oh.'

'Seriously, though...'

'Yes?'

'Truce, Rebecca?' he suggested.

'Truce,' she said on a sigh, surrendering her anger with the reluctance of someone shedding a protective garment.

They looked at each other. This kitchen wasn't very big, and feelings were still bouncing around in it like the aftershocks to an earthquake. Now that she *had* surrendered the feeling, she didn't want to think about how good it felt not to be angry with him any more.

Leaning back against the sink, he smiled at her lazily. 'So...staying for dinner?'

'What are you offering?' she returned.

The suggestive second meaning to the phrase hadn't been intentional and she winced inwardly. It was probably obvious that she'd take whatever he was offering very eagerly.

But he didn't comment on her unfortunate choice of words. Instead, his grin just widened, and a knowing light appeared in his dark eyes. 'I'm offering a drink first. White wine?'

'Lovely!'

'Then spaghetti with sauce from a jar and salad from a plastic bag,' he said. 'So the cooking's not much, but I promise I'll do a lot better with the entertainment. How does that sound?'

'Ask me again after I've experienced your performance.' Oh, no! Again!

And this time he echoed huskily, 'My...performance?'

'Yes.' She met his gaze head-on, and brazened her way out of the corner she'd painted herself into. 'Do you sing with perfect pitch? Play an instrument to concert standard?'

'The harp,' he shot back. 'Amazing what that does to the dexterity of your fingers. It comes in handy in…all sorts of situations…'

Abandoning any pretence about what was going on here, she discovered, as ninety-six-year-old Irene MacInerney obviously had, that it was delicious to flirt with Harry, delicious to be aware of him like this, knowing he was equally aware of her. He touched her frequently as they moved around the kitchen together, brushing an arm across her shoulder as he reached for the packet of spaghetti in a high cupboard, nudging her aside with a hand on her hip when he needed the sink.

By the time the pasta water was boiling, she was boiling too, with all the passion of her nature finding a compelling focus in this clamorous physical awareness of his flagrantly male form.

He hadn't bothered to put on a shirt. Had he simply forgotten? She certainly wasn't going to remind him! The sight of that chest of his, those shoulders, those arms, was just too good to resist, and she drank it in, with a possessive ache swelling by the minute inside her.

Oh, she wanted him! And he knew it, too, and was loving every betrayal of what she felt. Those betrayals came frequently, too. Her breathing quickened every time he touched her, and every time they got within inches of each other she found herself swaying towards him as if their attraction to each other was actually magnetic.

'The pasta will take ten minutes. I'd better go and put on a shirt,' he said at last.

'Don't,' came her instant reply. *Oh, Rebecca!*

'Can I possibly hope that's a compliment,' he teased softly, 'or are you just trying to save me the trouble of going upstairs?'

'Well, the stairs did look rather steep,' she answered, refusing to look at him because—as usual—her face gave everything away.

Kiss her now, Harry's inner man said impatiently, but he heroically delayed the gratification of the moment, knowing it would be all the better for being savoured like this, since it was wonderfully obvious that they both wanted it badly.

'My legs are pretty tired from tennis,' he drawled, 'so if you're sure you don't mind…'

'Quite sure,' she said, with a spinsterish look that didn't deceive him for a second. That glorious colour still flared in her cheeks, and her eyes were as big and dark as a cat's.

'Thank you,' he mouthed, deliberately making his lips mimic the form of a kiss.

She laughed. 'Harry, this is…'

'Nice?' he suggested blandly.

'*Very* nice!'

The pasta was spitting starchy water out onto the stove. He turned down the gas and managed to turn down his own heat to a sustainable level at the same time. Purely to keep himself from kissing her, he said, 'So, you said you'd run into Gareth at the hospital. Delivering babies, both of you?'

'Yes, I was covering for Grace—twice—because she was supposed to be away the whole weekend.' She frowned, and he saw it.

'*Supposed* to be?'

'Yes. Apparently they came back early. My second delivery turned into an emergency Caesarean, and Marcus was on hand so he did it. I was surprised to see him, and told him so— then wished I hadn't because he was in a pretty foul mood.'

'So why did they come back?' Harry asked.

Rebecca watched him as he went to the fridge to get out a bottle of vinaigrette dressing for the salad. Pottering about in the kitchen like this together, it felt so right and so natural…although there ought to be a law against what jeans did to a male rear end like Harry's.

'Well,' she answered slowly, as he closed the fridge again, 'Marcus said it was because their bed-and-breakfast turned out to be awful, but I can't believe that. Surely they'd just have gone elsewhere. To a motel, or something. It was a gorgeous day. I guess if it had been pelting rain I might have believed it, but…'

'No. Sounds odd, doesn't it?' he agreed. 'I've had a bad feeling about those two for a while now.'

'You mean…seriously bad?'

'Seriously bad,' he echoed. 'Grace isn't happy. I'm wondering if it all has something to do with the baby.'

'She said the baby was fine. I've been assuming it was her mother. She said they'd had a big fight over her marrying Marcus, and that she didn't want to make the first move towards reconciliation because her mother would only say "I told you so".'

'Which is a dead give-away, if you think about it,' he pointed out.

'"I told you so" because Grace *did* make a mistake in marrying Marcus?'

'It fits, doesn't it?'

'It does,' she had to agree. 'Oh, how sad…and horrible…for all four of them.'

'Four?'

'Grace. Marcus. Her mother. And there's a baby due in about two months, Harry.'

'Yes, there is, isn't there? I wonder how much that's contributing to the whole problem…'

By unspoken agreement, they let the subject drop. Without knowing more, there wasn't a lot to do to help. And Grace's bright reassurances, coupled with Marcus's black expression this morning, suggested that the couple themselves would not appreciate well-meant interference. Well, Grace had indicated exactly that in what she'd said about her mother.

Now the pasta had gone off the boil altogether. Harry fiddled with the gas again until it looked right, then turned to her. 'I estimate we've got five minutes.'

'Until…?'

He came towards her, laced his fingers together in the small of her back and bent towards her face. 'Until I have to take my mouth…away from yours…in order to put…spaghetti into it,' he answered, his lips blurred and soft against hers.

Better than last night. Quite definitely better. Last night she'd been drained and upset and not at all sure what she'd wanted beyond the immediate miracle of their joined mouths.

Tonight… Well, she'd had nearly twenty-four hours of living with the memory of his kiss, and somehow her feelings for him had deepened and grown roots with amazing speed in that time. It was like a hum in the air—a hum of understanding that she wanted more.

And, of course, last night he'd been wearing a sweatshirt.

His body was fabulous. Her hands couldn't get enough of it as she stroked the muscles and sinews of his back, then pushed him away just enough to rake her fingers through that absolutely kissable *edible* patch of hair in the middle of his chest, that she wanted to nuzzle.

He laughed, a low rumble that bubbled up to make him break away and squash his nose into her cheek. 'Rebecca, you're…'

'I'm what?'

'I don't know. So alive. I almost get the feeling you're quite enjoying this,' he whispered, and nibbled at her ear.

'Almost? Quite?'

'I love it, that's all. Your passion.'

'Egoist!'

'Not just your passion for…this,' he managed—just—as he swooped down to pull another kiss from her eager lips.

She wanted…fully intended…to pursue the point further, but his mouth was such a fabulous distraction that she couldn't. The subject stopped mattering and all that counted in the whole world was the fact that she was here in his arms, already so close to loving him that she doubted she would know when she crossed that invisible and all-important line.

'This is crazy, isn't it?' he said lazily.

'I know.'

'Not exactly a power career move—having a fling with the boss's daughter.' His voice was like a sensual caress, but she felt as if she'd been slapped. A 'fling', he'd phrased it. And she'd been flirting happily with the idea of future love.

'Is that how you see this?' she said painfully. 'As a bad career move, saved only by the fact that it's a fling and therefore *brief*?'

'Rebecca, I was—'

She didn't let him finish. 'Perhaps, from what you say, you might feel better about it if I promised to keep it a secret from Dad. Lots of lies and secretive comings and goings in the middle of the night. Would that help?'

Her icy tone left him in no doubt that she wasn't trying to be helpful.

'Rebecca, it was meant as a—'

'No. You've already sweet-talked me about your view on me working in the practice. I don't care if you *were* joking! Most jokes carry truth at their heart, and yours was no exception. You just can't get over the fact that I'm Marshall Irwin's daughter, can you? One way or another, you're going to make that into a problem, and you were doing that before you even met me.

'OK, well, you've convinced me now. It *is* a problem, whether we can't stand each other, or can't keep our hands off each other. We can't build a relationship—not a professional one, not a personal one—without my father and my work at the practice getting in the way, it seems, so let's not try. If Gareth Searle's got work to offer me at Southshore I'll take it, and the more hours the better.

'That seems like the only way we'll both get over this, without making things difficult for Dad. I'd better go,' she finished. 'And you'd better drain this pasta before it turns to mush.'

'I think you're overreacting.'

'*I* don't! You've got a problem with our relationship, Harry, and I'm not prepared to stick around while you try and solve it. I'm *not* a ''fling with the boss's daughter''. I'm me, and if you want me you'd better take that fact seriously!'

CHAPTER SEVEN

HARRY *did* want Rebecca.

He knew it once and for all the moment the door slammed resoundingly behind her. He loved the indignant blaze of her anger. His whole body crawled with need for her. And flings didn't enter into it. Foolish word, fling. He shouldn't have used it, although he *had* been joking.

She was probably right, though. Jokes usually were built around a kernel of truth.

If he'd been that seriously worried about Marshall's attitude, he should have found the strength to resist what Rebecca did to him. And if he didn't have the power to resist—and he certainly hadn't tonight—he needed to consider seriously what that meant. Protective fathers and professional careers aside, you couldn't pursue a woman like Rebecca Irwin without knowing what you really wanted.

With burning reluctance, he decided he had to somehow cool the fire inside him.

Prowling back into the kitchen, Harry looked at the spaghetti and found that his appetite for it had temporarily disappeared. Perhaps even permanently. The house seemed so full of Rebecca. Her intangible, exotic scent, her vibrant laugh, even the echo of her passionate movements.

He really didn't feel like being stuck at home, with their kisses and their angry words haunting the air like ghosts.

Pacing with restless impatience towards the phone on the coffee-table, he thumped down into the armchair beside it, then let his hand hover over the instrument. He still knew Phoebe Patterson's phone number off by heart, and he was sorely tempted to dial it.

Languid, beautiful, blonde Phoebe. She had been on the brink of a world-class modelling career before single motherhood had unexpectedly intervened. Harry had met her when her son Joad was four and Phoebe had been making a pretty decent living with commercials, voice-overs and small guest roles in soaps and police dramas.

With that sort of biography, she ought to have been a fascinating, vibrant person, but he'd gradually discovered that she hadn't been at all, because nothing—not her life, not her work, not the world at large—had excited her. Voice-overs had been 'dreary,' television shoots 'tedious'. A soft-drink commercial, in which she'd been seen—admittedly with some help from a stunt double—bungee jumping, windsurfing and hang-gliding had been 'mind-numbing, Harry, you can't *imagine*'!

And politics, the environment, the arts, travel and sport had all made her yawn or pout or fall asleep. Even little Joad, although she obviously loved him, had been frequently described, and in his own hearing, too, as '*mon petit* nuisance' or 'the B.R.A.T.', and she hadn't seemed to care much whether Harry had made friends with the boy or not. In any case, he'd almost always been left with Grandma when the two of them had gone out.

After three months, Harry just hadn't been able to stand the apathy and negativity any longer. He had been very careful about breaking off their relationship, but typically *that* hadn't touched her either.

'Well, it's been fun,' she'd said with a sigh, 'but... whatever. I didn't expect it to last.'

As he still saw her at tennis from time to time, he knew she'd had a new man on her arm within a week and had dated several others since. She was a very attractive woman, and knew it all too well. He wondered how she would react if he asked her out now for some night next week. She would be home, he was almost sure, carefully readying herself for the evening ahead.

A five-minute talk, and he'd probably have a date with her to look forward to. He picked up the phone, touched seven of the eight numbers, then dropped the receiver back in its cradle with an angry clatter.

'I can't do this,' he muttered aloud. 'When it really comes down to it, I don't care if I never see Phoebe again so what would a date with her solve? Nothing!'

Angrily, he shovelled an unwanted plateful of spaghetti into his mouth, then walked the long walk down into George Street in time to see a nine-thirty movie, not caring in the slightest that he was alone.

Saturday evening at seven was a terrible time to phone a man out of the blue, Rebecca knew. It was a dead give-away that you had nothing on for the evening, but she didn't care.

She was desperate, restless, *terrified*. Feeling like this about someone—about Harry—was just too dangerous, like a roller-coaster with loops and no safety bar. She'd thought, all these years, that she wanted a powerful love, but perhaps she had been wrong. Perhaps she was actually *afraid* to care and ache for someone the way Dad had cared for Mum.

'Oh, God, I don't want to analyse that now!' she muttered aloud, still alone in the house as Dad had not yet returned.

She'd had David Shannon's phone number in her address book for weeks and hadn't used it yet. Hadn't even been sure that she'd use it at all. She'd been through medical studies with David a couple of years ahead of her, and he'd gone out with another fellow medical student and a good friend of Rebecca's, Angie Kraus, for several months.

Angie and David had remained on good terms when they split up, and when Rebecca's move back to Sydney drew near, Angie had told her, 'I'll give you David's number. You remember, he moved up at the beginning of the year to do a urology registrarship at Royal Prince Alfred. Do contact him! I know he'd love to hear from you.'

Tonight, picking up the phone and checking the number in her book, Rebecca hoped very much that Angie had been right about this last bit, although it was quite likely that he wouldn't be home. If it came to saving face about ringing out of the blue on a Saturday night, she could always plead truthfully that she was on call.

The phone rang several times, and she was on the point of concluding that this was a waste of time when there was a click and a voice said, 'Hello?' It was him.

She muddled through a sentence or two of explanation. Angie had given her his number... The babies she'd been expecting this weekend had been safely delivered... It was probably an odd time to ring...

Then she realised that she didn't need to apologise. He was pleased to hear the sound of her voice, and said straight away, 'I know it's short notice but, if you haven't eaten, would you like to meet somewhere? Hate having nothing on for a Saturday.' He gave a self-conscious laugh. 'Doesn't usually happen. Your timing was perfect!'

The evening, unfortunately, wasn't. The Turkish food was nice, and so was David, but...

Inside Rebecca, the insidious knowledge licked at the edge of her mind that you could be terrified of something and still crave it, make the right decision with your brain and still succumb to what your body demanded.

Not yet willing to accept what all this meant, she agreed to another date with David and accepted his unthreatening goodnight kiss at the front door, not surprised when it failed to have any effect on her senses at all.

'How do you feel about it, Grace?' Marshall asked.

'Fine.' She put down her sandwich. 'I'm not ready to cut down my hours yet. If Rebecca herself is keen...'

'Oh, I am,' Rebecca answered immediately. *Very* keen since Saturday night. 'I like Dr Searle, and there's a lot of traffic through the health centre. I expect the variety and pace will be a good complement to the work here.'

They were discussing the plan for her to work three days at Southshore and two days at the practice. She and Dad had talked about it yesterday over breakfast, and he had been upset to find that she'd heard of the idea from Gareth Searle first. She'd admitted to him that it had been a shock initially, but hadn't told him how she'd rushed furiously over to Harry's full of accusations about his involvement in the proposal and his devious intentions.

After a solid night's sleep and a quiet day yesterday, the intensity of their response to each other on Friday and Saturday night now seemed like part of a particularly sensual and vivid dream, and she didn't know how to react to him now. There he was, sitting rather silently on the opposite side of Dad's office, his face closed, not meeting her gaze unless he had to.

She was equally reluctant to meet his.

She ought to have felt blessedly relieved. Hadn't she been mortally terrified by the strength of what she'd felt just two days ago? If she wasn't going to get close enough to Harry from now on to feel it again, so much the better. Subject closed!

'Gareth is keen for Rebecca to start as soon as possible,' Dad was saying. 'And I see no reason for any delay. The flexibility of the whole arrangement seems ideal for everyone, with what's going on at the moment with the housing development, so we may as well take advantage of that straight away. As I was telling Rebecca yesterday, he's hoping to have her cover their afternoon and evening hours from lunch until nine on Tuesdays and Thursdays, and a normal nine-to-five day on Wednesdays. So we'll have you on Mondays and Fridays, Rebecca. Or possibly covering the new Saturday morning hours when we put those in after Christmas.'

There really wasn't much else to discuss so the four doctors broke up and went in different directions on lunchtime errands. Rebecca took as little notice of Harry as she could, while still taking good care to avoid him, and she was able to hurry off to the bank without thinking about who would lock up, as Julie Cummings's blonde head was still bent over a list of supplies, checking them against the boxes which had just arrived from a drug company five minutes earlier.

After lunch, she recognised the wife of Harry's Olympic cycling hopeful in the waiting-room, here for her four-weekly pre-natal check with Grace. Both women were visibly larger since the last one.

'Here I am again already,' Lisa McNeill said.

Grace warned, 'And I'll be wanting you in every two weeks from now on.'

'Oh, good! That makes it seem closer. I'm getting impatient now that I'm starting to feel so big.'

'Yes…' Grace answered vaguely, and was about to usher her patient through when Harry came in and forestalled her.

'How's Shane?' he asked Lisa. 'Are the exercises helping?'

'He thinks so,' Lisa nodded. 'He's coming to see you again at the end of the week, so let's cross fingers you'll notice some improvement. He *has* to start cycling again because there's a competition carnival coming up soon.'

'Oh, yes?'

'Not a big one on the calendar, but it's a test, he feels, and if the knee gives him trouble it'll really start to throw him into doubt for the Olympics in 2000.' Her voice became husky suddenly. 'He wants it so badly, Dr Jones. Not as much as the baby, he says, and that's true, of course, but this has been such a healthy pregnancy that I'm starting to take that for granted, whereas his injuries have given him setback after setback over the past year. What will he do, if after all this work…?'

She couldn't finish.

'Come through, Lisa,' Grace said gently. 'When the baby's

born, it'll all fall into perspective for him. He'll see what's most important in his life. I believe that...'

There was an odd intensity to the statement.

The following day, Rebecca started at Southshore Health Centre. She hadn't thought very much about what it would be like. She hadn't had time to, after all. Yet, almost at once, she knew it had been the right decision.

With a rotating staff of up to five doctors at any one time, and a total of ten at the health centre altogether, there were frequent debates about trickier diagnoses and a large volume of patients coming through. As in a hospital internship, you really had to think on your feet.

By the end of the first week, she had to admit to herself that Harry had been closer to the truth than she'd ever deign to tell him. This stint at Southshore *would* be good for her professional standards, as well as her confidence.

When Grace came in for her pre-natal with Dr Julius Marr on Thursday afternoon, and Rebecca encountered her at the front desk, they greeted each other like long-lost cousins.

'It seems like more than three days,' Rebecca confessed.

'How is it going?'

'Good. Very good! I hope you're missing me!' *Idiot.* She chastised herself inwardly at this. You're not hoping she'll say something about Harry, are you?

'We are, actually,' Grace answered kindly.

'You didn't have to say that. I wasn't serious.'

'No, honestly! Because Harry brought in more of those Viennese chocolate biscuits of his, and with one less person to share them with, and Bev and Andrea both on diets, I'm eating *far* too many!'

She gave her warm laugh, then turned to greet tall, loose-limbed Julius Marr, who'd heard the confession about the biscuits.

'Better weigh you before we go any further,' he threatened darkly.

'Julius, don't be too severe, will you, but I do think I've gained about four kilos since last time,' Grace said with a wince.

It seemed like no time at all until Grace was back for her next check-up two weeks later, and again she was able to report to Rebecca afterwards that everything looked healthy and normal. 'No sign of gestational diabetes. My blood pressure's normal. My weight gain wasn't nearly as horrendous as I was afraid it would be.'

'I should think not!' Rebecca answered, accompanying her to the front desk to collect her next patient file. 'You look great, and you *should* be gaining at this stage. You're about thirty-three weeks now, aren't you?'

'Gee, you know how to say all the right things! Yes, I'm almost thirty-three weeks.'

'And I mean them, too.'

'Nice that *someone* does…' The cynical drawl was meant to be a joke, but it sat ill with Grace's round, open face and twinkling smile. And hadn't Rebecca and Harry agreed less than three weeks ago that most jokes contained a kernel of truth?

Grace left, and Rebecca felt her usual spurt of doubt and dissatisfaction at the brief exchange. Those tell-tale comments and expressions…and yet Grace blocked any attempts to help her or get her to air her problems openly. And, of course, if someone really didn't want to talk, you had to respect that.

She found that Julius Marr, too, was frowning as he watched Grace go.

'Do you know Marcus very well?' he asked Rebecca.

'No, hardly at all. We've met several times now, but he seems very reserved.'

'Very!' he agreed. 'Not that I know him well either, but we've spoken on the phone a couple of times about patients. I've heard nothing but praise for him as a doctor…'

There was a 'but' hanging in the air. It went unspoken,

however. Both of them had patients waiting. A mother and daughter, as it happened. The mother, Betty Reid, had rather advanced multiple sclerosis and was confined to a wheelchair so daughter Stephanie, a petite redhead in her late thirties, excused herself to Rebecca and wheeled her mother into Dr Marr's office, before coming next door to Rebecca's office for her own appointment.

'Look, I'm just here for a Pap,' she said to Rebecca as the door closed behind her. 'And Mum is having trouble with her speech at the moment so I wouldn't mind getting back to her as soon as we've finished here.'

She took off her black leggings as she spoke, and was soon lying on the examining table, her lower half covered by a paper sheet.

'It must be difficult for you to get out to the doctor,' Rebecca observed. 'Dr Marr would come and see your mother at home, wouldn't he?'

She was thinking of Dad's patient, Georgina Bennett, and his weekly visits to her at lunchtime or after work.

'Oh, he does.' Stephanie nodded, tensing a little as Rebecca inserted the metal speculum with her gloved hand.

'Just take some deep breaths,' Rebecca said. 'This is the icky part, isn't it?'

'I distract myself with relentless chatter on these occasions.' Stephanie laughed.

'Nearly done,' Rebecca promised, scraping some material from the cervix in two or three places and smearing it carefully onto one half of a clear glass slide, then taking a special brush and collecting some more cells from the opening of the cervix. These would fill the second half of the slide.

'But anyway,' Stephanie continued, 'Mum likes to get out sometimes so we make an excursion of it. We'll do some shopping together after this. She's not always as bad as she is at the moment. It's one of her exacerbation periods and, judging by previous episodes, we should see some improvement again soon. That, too, is only temporary, of course, but it helps us both.'

'Yes, I'm sure. It must be hard at the moment.'

'We take it as it comes.'

'All done now,' Rebecca said. She had sprayed the slide with a fixative and put it in its plastic box for transport to the pathology lab. Now she gently removed the speculum.

Stephanie sat up at once. 'No, Dr Marr is terrific,' she went on. 'I don't know what we'd do without him now!'

Oddly enough, Julius himself said exactly the same thing about Stephanie after Mrs Reid and her daughter had left. 'I don't know what Betty would do without Stevie.'

Rebecca smiled to herself. She liked Julius Marr a lot—he was dynamic, attractive, intelligent—but he definitely had his head up in the clouds at times. He obviously had no idea how much his voice gave away when he used Stephanie Reid's jazzy little nickname.

I wonder if she has any idea how he feels about her? Rebecca mused. I wonder if *he* has any idea himself!

This idle observation should *not* have brought her thoughts immediately to the subject of Harrison Jones, but somehow it did. They'd hardly seen each other since she'd started dividing her time between Dad's practice and the health centre. Their different hours only coincided on Fridays and Mondays, and even then Harry had twice been out, seeing patients at the local nursing home. Rebecca was now in the perverse situation of wishing she'd see him more often so that she'd get more opportunity to convince him—and herself—that she had no desire to see him at all!

Fate was evidently conspiring to help her in this regard, therefore, when Dad suggested on Friday night at dinner that she join him and Harry in a game of golf on Saturday afternoon.

'Dad, I *loathe* sport!' That was her first reaction. Not strictly true. 'Any sport that Harry Jones was involved in' would have been more accurate.

'Golf isn't sport,' Dad returned serenely. 'It's Zen—a spiritual experience. And you used to play with me all the time when you were eighteen.'

'Yes, and I haven't played since. Besides, doesn't Harry play tennis?'

Coming back from which he then has a shower and doesn't put on a shirt until his hair is dry...

'Oh, Harry will play anything.' There *wasn't* a sexual double entendre in those words. Dad hadn't intended one. So why did it leap out at Rebecca?

'Not so much because he's a sports nut,' Dad went on, 'although he does like to keep fit with those ocean swims of his every morning, but because he likes to think about it from a professional point of view. Which muscle groups are most at risk? How can playing better reduce the likelihood of injury? That sort of thing. I persuaded him he needed to give golf a try as an educational experience.'

'So he doesn't really play either?'

'No. Which is exactly why it would be good if you came.'

'What, so I can play worse than he does and take the pressure off his ego?'

'Precisely! You're so refreshingly *exact* at times, Rebecca.'

'Honestly, *men*!' She scraped her chair back irritably and began to gather up the dishes.

Dad was laughing, sitting back comfortably in his chair and having a really good laugh. Maddening! She glared at him and he laughed harder.

'All right, I'll come!' she vowed rashly. 'And I'll play to win!'

She lost abysmally, of course. If golf was Zen, as Dad had claimed, then she had the worst possible approach and attitude to the game, playing in a white-hot fury against the male sex in general and Harrison Jones in particular. Damn his ego!

She hoped to crush it beneath the metal head of this odd-looking club, whatever it was called.

She flattered herself, however, that she wasn't letting her mood show.

The righteous flush in her cheeks and the dew of effortful sweat on her brow could be put down to the hot afternoon. It was November now, and summer was indulging in a preview season this year.

The harder she tried, of course, the more *off* course went her ball. There it was, sailing into the pretty curved shape of the sand trap yet again while Dad and Harry already had their balls on the green.

'Back luck, Rebecca,' the latter said to her this time.

'Oh, I like the sand,' she responded extravagantly. 'It's a *challenge*.'

'Let's see if I can give you some suggestions,' Dad said heartily, and followed her to the grassy edge of the sand trap. 'Gypsy,' he added in an undertone, as soon as they were out of Harry's hearing, 'there's no need to play *that* badly. Harry's ego is doing very well at the moment.'

'Dad, I'm not playing this badly on purpose!'

'Oops! Then perhaps for the sake of *your* ego, I'd better let Harry go on thinking that you are. He's been quite touched at your endeavours so far.'

'*Touched!*' she shrieked.

And she didn't know which was worse—to have Harry thinking she cared enough about his feelings to play like this deliberately, or to have him know that it was the best she could seriously do.

At some point several years down the track, she'd probably look back on this scene—the glorious weather, the distant views of parks, the airport and red-roofed houses, Dad and Harry chatting amicably in between apparently effortless putts and drives, and herself getting more and more dishevelled, in a state of suppressed frenzy—and laugh.

Today, it wasn't funny at all. Today, all the angry, aching complexity of her feelings for Harry churned around inside her and erupted forth to produce the worst golf score since the game was invented. The only thing she could possibly do was carry it off with carelessness and humour.

'So, Dad, confess, please. How exactly did you get the magnet into my ball?' she asked him after nine putts on the seventeenth hole had failed to sink her ball. And on the eighteenth, when the torture was finally over, she said, 'Does the clubhouse here have a trophy room? They may wish to include my record-breaking scorecard amongst their exhibits, don't you think?'

Tossing Harry a brilliant, shallow smile, she found that he was watching her, wearing an expression of quiet appreciation, and she flushed for about the twentieth time that day.

He looked so casually, heart-stoppingly gorgeous in his cream knit shirt and baggy navy shorts that it actually made her weak at the knees to look at him. And if she let herself think of the times they'd kissed... The word seemed hugely inadequate, she decided, as Dad and Harry indulged in a short post-mortem on the game.

There had been a totality and a completeness to the moments she'd spent in Harry's arms that needed a whole new vocabulary—one that she just didn't possess. Instead, the memory simply bathed her again as she stood there, like a cascade of warm syrup.

I didn't know it was possible to ache for a man this way, to feel my...my bones humming...

'Is that it, then?' she drawled deliberately, taking advantage of a silence from the two men. 'Do we get to go home now?'

'Rebecca!' Dad protested. 'You're just rusty, that's all. You'll soon get your eye and your swing back again.'

'I won't,' she answered, 'because I'm not playing again. So there!'

Harry was laughing now, a deep, lazy sort of sound. For

the effect it had on her, it may as well have been a caress, and his eyes were raking over her, alight with amusement…and heat. If Dad hadn't been busy rearranging his clubs in their bag, he'd have noticed in a flash.

She wanted to tell Harry, You can't look at me that way! I'm not in the market for flings. For a start, it'd be a sheer waste of the amount of heat we generate. Not to mention the fact that I consider myself to be worth just a little *more* than that!

She couldn't tell him any such thing, of course, and certainly not now, so she *looked* it at him instead—a proud, fiery glare which, she was extremely satisfied to note, stripped that hot look from his face and had him turning away with a dissatisfied grimace.

Good! He'd evidently got the message!

Then, to her chagrin, she heard Dad proposing a drink at the clubhouse, followed by dinner somewhere. More time in Harry's company was the last thing she needed, but crying off was out of the question. Ten minutes later, they were at a table by the window in the members' bar, overlooking the course. No hope of even a temporary escape either as Dad had been the one to go off to buy the drinks.

'I take it you wouldn't have suggested this yourself?' Harry said at once. If it had been any other man, she might have relished the way he got straight to the point.

'No,' she agreed, just as bluntly. 'I'd have gone home.'

'Whereas, surprisingly enough, I'm looking forward to the prospect of an evening out with you.'

'Don't,' she told him. 'Because I'm planning to be bad company.'

'*Planning?*'

'Harry, we can't seem to stay friends for more than a few hours at a stretch. You said you wanted a, quote, *fling*.'

'No, I said I—'

She didn't let him finish. 'Well, aside from the fact that

''flings'' are not my style, I'd find any relationship with you, no matter how it was defined, far too much of a nuisance, I think, to be worth the trouble.'

'A *nuisance*?'

'Yes. We clash, Harry. Haven't you noticed?'

'How could I fail to?' he muttered dryly.

'That's wearing, and difficult, and time-consuming, and I'm not interested. You like things out in the open. Have I stated my case clearly enough?'

'With bells on!' he retorted coolly. 'Some might say you've not merely *stated* it, you've pushed me into it face down and ground your boot heel against the back of my head.'

'Right, well, good,' she finished lamely. 'I intended to. At least, nothing to do with my heel and the back of your head, but—'

'You were eager to get your point across?' he suggested helpfully.

'Yes.'

She felt completely miserable for the rest of the evening. How did he *do* this to her? She was actually *frightened*, still, at how much she wanted him, to the point where she'd hidden behind belligerent, exaggerated phrases which would have put any reasonable man off for good.

Since, in fact, this was the aim of the exercise, why was she feeling so remorseful about it now? And since when had she been this changeable, this unsure of herself?

There had only been one other time in her life when she'd felt this churned up over a man. Matt, whom she'd almost slept with, several years ago in Melbourne. After going out with him for two months, she'd been within five minutes of climbing into his bed when she'd overheard him discussing the imminent conquest with his male flatmate in the crudest possible terms. She'd confronted him at once, then walked out and never seen him again, and hadn't got that close to a man since.

The turmoil she felt about Harry now, for very different reasons, was much, much worse.

All she wanted was to crawl home, put her head under a pillow and stay that way until the violent storm of her physical response to him had spent itself—which it surely must, eventually—so that she could return to a livable existence again.

CHAPTER EIGHT

'AND you'll go and see Georgina Bennett at lunchtime,' Dad finished, his voice a faint, laboured croak.

'You don't want Harry to do that?' Rebecca queried, looking down at the blanket-wrapped form on the bed.

Dad had a bad dose of spring flu, with aches and fever and shivers and sweats, a sore throat, a stuffy head and a rasping chest. Coming to work was out of the question, and he hadn't even argued when Rebecca had told him so.

'No,' he croaked once more in answer to her question. 'She told me last week she'd like to meet you.'

'OK, then. I'd like to meet her, too. Anything else, Dad?'

'No…' He waved her away. 'Just want to sleep.'

'There's iced juice and plain water, and a Thermos of chicken broth and one of tea right here by your bed, as well as flu tablets and cough medicine,' she informed him. 'And tissues and the thermometer.'

'Thanks. Now, go, gypsy, and don't be late.'

'Look after yourself, Dad. Keep your fluids up, and take your temperature if you start to feel any hotter.'

'I'm a doctor, too, remember,' he managed to joke.

On reaching the surgery, Rebecca reported to everyone, 'It's just a bout of flu. His temperature's not high enough for any real concern, and it's not pneumonia because I made him let me listen to his chest!'

'You managed to get on to Grace?' Harry asked.

'Yes, last night. He was still saying then that he'd be fine, but I knew he wouldn't. Grace is coming in.'

'Here she is now,' said Bev, as the pleated blind on the door rattled.

'Sorry,' said the pregnant doctor breathlessly.

'You're not late, Grace,' Harry soothed.

'How is he, Rebecca?'

'Sick enough to actually admit to the fact,' she answered.

'The pity of it is that it's his birthday on Sunday, isn't it, Rebecca?' Deirdre said.

'Yes,' she answered, 'but he didn't feel that fifty-one was much to celebrate so he hasn't planned anything. He's going to Melbourne next weekend for my old obstetrics professor's daughter's wedding. This is his third wedding this year! So he's actually pleased to be laid low now rather than then.'

'Still.' Deirdre pulled a face. 'I made him a cake last night.' She gestured to a white cardboard box sitting on her desk.

'Oh…!' There was a groaned chorus of disappointment.

Harry asked, 'What's the protocol, gang? Do we eat it without the guest of honour? Or does Rebecca take it home to him?'

'The two of us'll never get through a whole cake before it goes stale,' Rebecca said. 'He's barely managing weak tea and chicken broth at the moment, in any case. Deirdre, I think it's up to you.'

'We'll eat it at lunchtime, and you can take him home what's left,' the efficient receptionist decided. 'Not much of a celebration, but I hate waste!'

There was a chorus of approval at the decision…possibly tinged with a little guilt.

'I've been thinking about his birthday too,' Harry said next. 'Would he like a kitten, Rebecca? My parents had an injured one brought in last week and they've patched him up but no one's claimed him. He's about three months old so he'll be all right on his own during the day. The people who found him have said they'll pay the bill and keep him themselves rather than see him put down, but they'd prefer it if another home could be found for him. What do you think?'

'Dad does miss our old Gussy,' Rebecca answered. 'We

both do. And he's got a very soft heart when it comes to injured animals. Yes, I think he'd love a kitten for his birthday.'

'Oh, it'll be gorgeous!' Bev said. With her desk covered in pictures of her children and grandchildren and pets, plump, motherly Bev was unashamedly sentimental. 'Will you put a red bow around his neck and have him in a cute little basket?'

'Oh, probably.' Rebecca laughed. 'He is a birthday present, after all, isn't he?'

'Want to come over to my parents' tonight after work, then, and pick him up?' Harry asked.

She didn't want to at all, of course, but how could she say that in front of Deirdre and Bev and Julie and Grace? It had been such a casual, practical invitation, in any case, that it surely wouldn't be too awkward to get through.

'Sounds good,' she said.

'I'll pick you up at eight, shall I?'

'Great…'

With four pairs of female eyes and four pairs of female ears close at hand, Rebecca hoped she didn't sound as reluctant as she felt. But the idea of spending any time alone with Harry these days made her insides churn in a way she wasn't prepared to accept.

As soon as the last of the morning's patients left, three and a half hours later, she drove over to the Bennetts' house. She'd been told about the car repairs in the back yard and Georgina's increasingly effortful crochet-work, but it was still quite moving to be plunged amongst this brave, easygoing family who were managing so well.

Georgina didn't have her crochet-work in her lap today, and she was slumped in an armchair on her favourite enclosed veranda. She wore a pink velour dressing-gown, a cotton nightdress and slippers, as if dressing had been too much effort, and her hair was scraped back into an ugly knot.

Rebecca wasn't surprised to find her this way. Wayne

Bennett had given the thumbs-down sign as he'd met her at the top of the drive and accompanied her into the house, and Frank Bennett had already been inside, standing at the kitchen stove with an opened tin of soup in his hand.

'Dr Irwin? Nice to meet you. Trying to make her eat, but she doesn't want to,' he'd added in an undertone.

'So this is Rebecca!' Catching sight of her, Georgina summoned enough energy to smile, and immediately called to her husband to make tea. 'Gee, you look like your dad!'

'Do I? Not many people tell me that.'

'Yes, you do,' Georgina insisted, the words dragging from her with effort. 'Your eyes and your smile, which are what I always notice.'

'You don't look as if *you're* smiling much today,' Rebecca said.

'Well, no, I'm not,' Georgina agreed with a sigh. 'One of my crook days.'

'Mr Bennett says you don't feel like eating.'

Georgina shrugged. 'I'll try to manage something. But, look at me, I've swelled up again. It feels terrible. And my waterworks are playing up.'

'You mean you're not passing much?'

'No. It's all gone into my ankles and my hands.'

She did look very puffy, which explained the absence of the crochet-work. Her fingers probably didn't have the dexterity at the moment.

'This is the sort of thing you've had before, isn't it?' Rebecca asked.

'Oh, yes, it comes and goes. I'd been pretty good lately. Always forget how rotten this feels! Doctor, I'm just getting real bloody sick of it, if you want the truth.'

'I know.' Rebecca nodded helplessly, wondering if Dad would have had something better to say than this, something more concrete and useful to offer. 'I know,' she repeated. 'Look, I'll prescribe a diuretic. That should take the swelling down and help with your waterworks. Dad's got flu today, unfortunately. I've ordered him to bed for the whole weekend. I know you probably wish—'

'I'm sure you're just as good as your dad, love.' With an effort, Georgina leaned forward and patted Rebecca's hand with her own uncomfortably swollen one. 'Just as long as I get my script for the tablets.'

Rebecca stayed for another ten minutes, writing out the precious prescription and checking all the usual things. Blood sugar still too high. Bowels still giving a lot of trouble.

'Here's your soup, gorgeous,' Frank Bennett said to his wife, just as Rebecca was ready to leave. 'I've made you some toast soldiers to dip in it, too, so get to work, OK, beautiful, before you fade away to a shadow. Thanks, Doctor,' he added to Rebecca in an aside, then said to his elder son, Brian, who'd just entered the house, 'Walk Dr Irwin to her car, would you, mate?'

'No worries,' nodded the dark, good-looking twenty-four-year-old.

But Brian had plenty of worries, which tumbled out as soon as they were out of his mother's hearing. 'Is it just going to go on like this? Mum's great, but she's getting so sick of it. Is there ever going to be a cure?'

'Oh, Brian, one day,' Rebecca answered. 'That's what we all hope, isn't it? Medical research is constantly working to try and understand SLE better, but—' she had to be honest '—I doubt there'll be any significant breakthroughs in time to help your mother. We just have to keep going with what we've got now.'

'Yeah, OK,' he agreed. 'Still, this bad patch'll end eventually, and she'll feel a lot better then. That's how it always goes.'

Back at the surgery, Harry knew Rebecca had been to see Georgina and asked her about it as she stood in the little kitchen, making herself some tea and heating some leftovers in the microwave for her lunch.

'Not very good at all today,' she had to reply. 'Apparently it's part of her normal cycle of exacerbations and remissions, but if I hadn't known that...' She shrugged.

'You might have packed her off to hospital?' Harry suggested.

'Probably.'

'The disease does have a gradual downward course. What you saw today would have been part of that.'

'I know. But I'll get Dad to make an extra visit as soon as he's back on board.'

'I'll do it, if you like, if Marsh isn't back by Monday.'

'Thanks. I'll take you up on that,' she answered, forgetting about the tension and uncertainty that existed between them. It had no place in anything that involved patients.

'Not doubting your judgement, are you, Rebecca?' His tone took away any suggestion that he thought she *should* have such doubts.

And she wasn't. Not really. 'Just wishing there was more that could be done. As are her husband and sons.'

'Hate it when you can't pull that miracle rabbit from your medical hat?'

'Exactly!'

'I've been thinking,' Harry said now. 'If you want to stay with your dad tonight, we can get the kitten tomorrow or Sunday instead. Now that my parents know he's going to you two, they won't mind keeping him longer.'

'No, Dad hates being pestered when he's sick,' Rebecca answered. 'He'd rather be left alone, and not have me fussing around. Let's leave the arrangement as it is.'

He nodded. 'Whatever suits you.'

There was something guarded in his voice and body language suddenly as he loped casually from the room. It was nearly a week since last Saturday's memorable game of golf, and today was the first time they'd seen each other for more than a few seconds in passing. What she'd said to him in the clubhouse had given him no encouragement to think of something like a kitten for her father's birthday.

He could have punished her a lot harder than he had for her blunt words, and yet he wasn't. There was no aggression or hostility emerging from that dense, athletic frame, only the guardedness which was, surely, just what she'd asked for.

Hugging her arms around herself to suppress a sudden, reasonless shiver, Rebecca went into her office to eat a hurried and solitary lunch, wondering why she was so dissatisfied with her own responses lately.

'Oh, he's just *gorgeous*!' Rebecca said, taking the half-grown ball of tabby-striped fur into her arms.

'His stitches are still a bit sore,' Peter Jones said, 'so be careful around his left hind leg. He was lucky it didn't break, but he did have quite a gash there when the Meads brought him in.'

'What happened to him?'

'Well, we don't know. It didn't look as if he'd been savaged by a dog—no obvious bite marks. They found him injured in the gutter so it was probably a car or a motorbike. Whoever it was, though, either hadn't noticed or hadn't cared enough to bring him in. His body temperature had dropped dangerously by that time, and we only just pulled him through.'

'Poor little muffin,' she crooned. 'Oh, you're *purring* for me! Oh, thank you!' She remembered how Gus had tried to purr for her in Harry's car during his last minutes of life, and that he hadn't quite had the strength. This little tabby puss, just starting out in life, had been found near death too, but he'd been luckier. He was going to be fine, and it felt *right* to have him…not quite to replace Gus, but to make up for his loss.

She looked up, still smiling, to find that Harry was watching her as he stood at his father's side, and there it was again. Sheer magnetism, which she was helpless to do anything about.

'Now, Harry says you stopped at a supermarket on the way here and got food for him, and you have a basket and a blanket at home?'

'Yes, which I've washed since Gus used it.'

'Cats have sensitive noses. He'll probably find some animal smell still lingering around the house, but at this age it won't upset him. Now, he's used to a litter tray...'

'Yes, we got some litter, too, and I have a plastic tub to put it in.'

'And here's a cardboard cat box to transport him in. Since we didn't know anything about his history, I've given him a cat flu injection and a worm tablet, and he'll need the follow-up flu injections at one-month intervals. And it's probably not necessary to say this, since I'm sure you have a responsible attitude to cat ownership, but do get him desexed before six months, won't you?'

'Definitely! We live across from Centennial Park, and the last thing I'd want is to have him fathering a new generation of feral cats there.'

'All set, then!'

'Oh, Peter, you can't let them go off without a cup of tea!' Rhonda said, coming through from the private part of the house. 'And I've got lemon cake, too, Harry.'

'Lemon cake? How can I resist?' he teased.

'Seriously, though...'

'Seriously, it's up to Rebecca.'

All three members of the Jones family turned to look at her with their brown eyes, which gave her little choice. 'I'd love a cup of tea,' she agreed weakly.

So they all trooped through to the living-room, which contained an eccentric mix of chairs and couches, upholstered in different fabrics which should have clashed but somehow didn't. Peter immediately slumped into the deepest and squish-iest of the seating options with a grunt of fatigue and relief, Harry began to prowl and Rhonda said brightly, 'I'll pop the kettle on…'

'I'll help,' Rebecca offered promptly, wanting to get away from Harry for reasons which she firmly refused to dwell upon.

She regretted her offer once alone in the kitchen with Harry's mother, however, as the latter was well imbued with maternal instinct when it came to her son bringing the same woman to the house *twice*, even if both times it had been on legitimate cat-orientated business.

Not that her questions were in any way pointed. She was much too well mannered and just plain nice for that, but… Well, it wasn't something you could put into words. Rebecca knew that Rhonda was wondering what role she filled in Harry's life, was probably concluding it was something sig-nificant and was already in the process of trying to decide how she felt about it.

And the really crazy thing about it, Rebecca thought, is that I want her to feel *great* about it! Which is idiotic when I feel terrible about it myself, and when there's nothing going on in any case…

It didn't change either as they sat in the lounge-room with their tea and cake, only this time Harry's father jumped on the bandwagon as well. Men were perhaps quicker at making up their minds in these situations. He was soon beaming at her, as if there'd just been an engagement announcement, and the atmosphere of expectancy was so palpable that Harry actually apologised for it as soon as they were alone with Muffin in the car.

'Sorry about all that…' The fact that he didn't bother to explain what he was saying sorry *for* wasn't exactly reassur-ing.

Rebecca's fount of conversation dried up completely, and

all she could think about was the fact that here she was again, alone with Harry—kittens didn't count—and aching for him, with no idea how to act on the unwanted, frightening feeling or how to make it go away.

'Lovely!' Dad rasped from his bed. 'Will he stay and keep me warm? Oops, no, he's lively, wants to go exploring. The red ribbon was a nice touch, gypsy, but let's take it off now. Look at him, he's pawing at it. I don't think he likes it. Now, does he have a name?'

'He's your birthday present, Dad.' She and Harry had decided against saving the gift until Sunday. Ill though Dad was, he'd probably notice a miaowing voice and the sound of wild kitty paws thudding down the corridor. 'You need to name him,' Rebecca finished, and Harry, standing in the background with his hands thrust deep in the pockets of his old jeans, nodded agreement.

'You don't expect any inspiration on that score tonight, I hope!' Dad responded.

'We can wait a few days.'

'No, at three months he's been too long without a name already. I'll delegate the task to you.'

'Well, I did call him a poor little muffin at one stage so I started thinking of him as Muffin in the car.'

'Muffin. OK, we'll go with Muffin. Are you staying for a bit, Harry?'

'Better head off, I think,' he answered, and, as happened far too often, there was something in his tone that made Rebecca's glance flick automatically towards his face.

What she saw there echoed the full complexity of her own feelings and she thought miserably, He's as resistant to this heat between us as I am. He doesn't want it. I don't want it. Why won't it *go away*?'

'I'll see you out,' she muttered, and they walked in silence down the stairs.

Reaching the door first, she held it open for him, then stood back so he could go through without any risk of an accidental touch. 'Thanks,' she said, 'for thinking of the kitten. Dad was really pleased, even if he was too ill for it to show.'

'It did show,' Harry countered. 'I think I'm reasonably good at picking up signals, even if they're not put into words.'

Hell! She flinched and his insides seemed to cave in. He hadn't meant it as a reference to their own relationship, but it had come out that way and she was as aware of the double meaning as he was.

That was the last thing he wanted at the moment, when all he aimed for in their dealings with each other was that they get through each exchange without him burning for her with such need that cold showers—*frequent* cold showers, on top of his cold morning swim—did absolutely nothing. And, if that wasn't bad enough, he was starting to understand that the physical part of what he felt was the least of the problem.

'Anyway...' he growled now, with no clear idea in the least about what he was saying. 'No need for thanks at all. The opposite. My parents were grateful to you for taking the little guy, and so am I. I'll see you soon, OK?'

'OK, Harry. Goodnight.'

She closed the door between them, and as he reached the front gate he imagined her gusting out a shaky sigh and fighting to still the tremble of physical need in her body, just as he was doing.

On Sunday morning, Dad was still feeling too ill to stir from bed and hadn't managed to finish his single slice of toast. Rebecca had already exacted from him the promise of another day in bed, so when the phone rang at half past eight she vowed not to disturb him with the call, no matter who it was.

But when she heard Frank Bennett give his name...

'Georgina can't get her breath, Doctor. It's like breathing underwater, she says. And the swelling's got even worse.'

Breathing underwater...all that swelling...kidney failure.

But she'd been right. There was no point in disturbing Dad for something like this.

'Get her to hospital, Mr Bennett. Straight away. I'll...I'll meet you there.'

It was a foolish promise, really. There would be nothing she could do. Georgina Bennett would be in the hands of doctors far more experienced with such an emergency than Rebecca was. She would be given a powerful diuretic intravenously, and have her potassium level measured. She'd be assessed for kidney dialysis and probably be placed on a dialysis machine this afternoon. None of this was Rebecca's province at all. Still, she felt responsible.

And to blame? she wondered as she drove down Anzac Parade towards Southshore Hospital. 'Should I have seen this coming on Friday, with the swelling and loss of appetite?'

The half-hour she spent with the Bennetts passed in a jumble of questions and waiting and more questions, then there was nothing more she could usefully do. She'd explained to the family what was going on, and spoken to the specialist, telling him all she knew of Georgina's history and current problems.

'We'll let you know, shall we?' he offered. 'If anything changes?'

'Yes, please.'

The phone call came sooner than she expected, at five in the afternoon, when she'd just got home from a late and chemistry-less lunch with David Shannon and had tiptoed upstairs to find Dad asleep, as he'd been for most of the morning.

Mrs Bennett had died, renal specialist Liam Reilly told her, of heart failure during dialysis. The family were with her now, and all the arrangements were in hand.

'Thanks for letting me know,' Rebecca said uselessly, and put down the phone.

She couldn't stay in the house. Dad was still asleep. Instead, an instinct and a need which she didn't stop to analyse took her straight out to the car and into a moderate swell of traffic coming home from the beach. Several minutes later, she was in Harry's street and driving past his house.

Like the other terrace houses in the street, it gave away little to the passerby—no hints as to whether its occupant was out or at home even, let alone any clue as to what he might be doing or what sort of welcome she'd receive if she turned up at his door and told him— Impossible. She couldn't possibly confront him in this state, with a childish demand for reassurance.

I *know* it's not my fault. I know it's just the way things happen. Georgina herself would have said that. And it's part of the profession I chose. I can't expect anyone—not Harry, not Dad—to provide me with pat answers and easy reassurances on a bad day. The Bennetts have lost their wife and mother. Dad's lost a patient he cared about. Let me go home, see if he's awake yet and give him the news as best I can.

Rebecca was to have her mettle tested in this way again just five days later. This time, however, although it still wasn't truly her own sorrow, it was even worse.

'The baby's pounding me to pieces,' said Lisa McNeill at ten-thirty on Friday morning, coming out of Grace's office after her routine pre-natal. 'Only another five weeks of it, thank goodness. Girl or boy, I'd say this one's going to be an athlete like Shane! Bye, Dr Gaines.'

She stopped at the front desk to make another appointment for the next week, leaving just as Grace herself came down the corridor in search of her next patient.

There was something odd about Grace's manner. Rebecca noticed it at once, and put down the file she'd just picked up, swallowing back the patient's name that had been on her lips.

'Everything OK, Grace?' she asked.

The place was quiet this morning. Dad had been well

enough to come to work by Monday morning, and had attended Georgina Bennett's funeral on Tuesday, but early this morning he'd flown to Melbourne for a long weekend centred around his friend's daughter's wedding. Harry wasn't here either, as he was visiting some patients at Hazel Cleary Lodge. He was due back any minute.

Grace was holding her fingers lightly against her bulging abdomen, the colour had drained from her face and she was concentrating intensely. She didn't answer Rebecca's question.

'Is it the baby?' Rebecca persisted. She didn't need to calculate dates. Lisa McNeill had just reminded her. Grace had five weeks to go. Premature, yes, but these days there was a near hundred per cent chance that the baby would be fine.

'Come into my office, Rebecca,' Grace said at last in a strange tone.

'What's wrong?' Rebecca demanded more urgently, as soon as the door had closed behind her. This whole thing was starting to alarm her now. Grace looked terrible.

'What Lisa said.' She was still splaying her fingers over her abdomen. 'About the baby kicking her to pieces. I'm trying to think. I—I can't remember when I last felt my baby move.'

She was starting to shake now.

'We'll get the Doppler out,' Rebecca said, a hollow feeling opening in her stomach, though she tried to remain professionally calm. 'Listen for the heartbeat.'

'Yes,' Grace nodded. 'I mustn't panic.'

But she was.

'Lie down, Grace, and lift up your dress.' Rebecca plugged in the device as she spoke. Amplifying the sound of the foetal heartbeat, it would provide more dramatic and convincing reassurance than a stethoscope or the ambiguous sensations of slight movement.

Grace was forcing herself to breathe normally. 'Wednesday night. There was movement on Wednesday night. I remember, because Marcus said—' She stopped.

Rebecca had the microphone-like instrument on her stomach now, and Grace's own heartbeat, half the speed of the baby's, was coming through clearly, as were her normal digestive sounds. There was a background hiss and crackle, too. Nothing else.

'I'll move it lower,' Rebecca said, but again no rapid foetal heartbeat sounded to compete against Grace's.

They both went on listening as Rebecca moved the instrument from one spot to another, but it was no good. There was no heartbeat, and with the baby just five weeks from birth there was no doubt about what this meant.

Grace had not moved from the table. She lay inert, with one hand shielding her eyes, although she hadn't yet cried. Rebecca knew there was nothing she could say or do that would help. Instead, wordlessly, she took Grace's other hand between both of hers and pressed it, and they both stayed that way for a minute that seemed to last for ever.

Finally, Rebecca said quietly, 'I'll ring Marcus, Grace.'

'No!' Her voice was harsh and strident. 'I don't want Marcus. I want Mum!'

Shaken by the vehemence of the words and the tone, Rebecca could only mumble, 'All right.'

Grace sat up at last—she looked like a ghost—and said, 'My address book is in my bag. The number's there. Under K. Kent, my maiden name. It just says ''Mum'', but her name is Margaret.'

'OK, I have it.'

She left the room at once, to find Harry in the waiting-room and Deirdre and Bev getting edgy.

'Nothing wrong, is there?' Deirdre asked in an undertone at once, leaning close so that her striped blouse brushed Rebecca's arm. 'Where's Grace?'

There was no point in trying to soften the truth. 'She's lost the baby *in utero*,' Rebecca said. 'She realised she hadn't felt any movement since Wednesday, and when we listened we picked up her heartbeat but not the baby's. I'm afraid there's no doubt. She wants me to ring her mother. And one of us will need to drive her to Southshore so they can induce labour.'

'But what about Marcus?' Bev said. 'He could come and get her. Surely—'

'She doesn't want Marcus,' Rebecca had to report. 'She wants her mother.'

The next half-hour was terrible. Grace's mother, Margaret Kent, was in tears on the phone, and so upset that Rebecca had to urge her to take a taxi if she couldn't calm herself enough to drive. Deirdre and Bev had to apologise to waiting patients. They'd quickly decided to explain that Dr Gaines had been taken ill. Several people, fortunately, had routine problems and elected to reschedule their appointments for another time. Harry, meanwhile, would see as many people as he could, while Bev phoned those of Grace's patients that she could reach and Rebecca took Grace to hospital.

They were all wondering what could have gone wrong. Rebecca knew that cord strangulation was the most likely explanation. It happened in a small percentage of healthy pregnancies. But today that cold statistic she'd learned during her obstetric diploma seemed particularly cruel.

Grace said little on the short journey to the hospital, and Rebecca dealt with as many of the formalities of admission for her as she could. She was a little relieved that at least Grace was given the most secluded of the delivery rooms, far from the nursery and from the sounds of women labouring to produce a living child.

'I'll be in here for a couple of days, I suppose,' Grace said when she was gowned and in bed. 'I'll send Mum home to bring some things.'

There was a numb, distant quality to her manner now, and Rebecca realised that Grace was trying not to think about the reality of this. She blurted aloud, 'Can't I contact Marcus for you? He may even be here…'

But, as it had been in her office, Grace's reply was sharp and immediate. She shook her head so that her halo of newly cut red-brown curls fluffed out. 'No! I won't see him! Our marriage is over, and it's taken this to make me realise it. I'll be moving out of the house as soon as I can. Perhaps I should have done it months ago!'

'Oh, Grace…'

'You need to get back to work, Rebecca.' Her voice, once again, was harsh, and Rebecca realised that she didn't want to talk about anything now.

A nurse had arrived to put up a drip, and she reported, 'Dr Marr will be here to see you soon. He wants you to think about an epidural.'

'No.' Grace shook her head firmly. 'I'd like to try a natural birth.'

She was gearing up for the hard and futile work of labour. Rebecca squeezed her hand once more and left, knowing there'd be a huge backlog of patients by now.

As she'd anticipated, she and Harry worked all day to catch up and fit in those of Grace's patients who couldn't be contacted or cancelled. They missed lunch and still had a full waiting-room by late afternoon.

It wasn't easy, and the times when everyone managed to forget Grace in order to focus on the needs of patients were actually the best.

I'm glad it's Harry, Rebecca found herself thinking. I'm glad it's the two of us here today.

He touched her or said a quick word every time their paths crossed, and those tiny moments were so intensely nourishing that they actually made her ache.

No news came from the hospital, and by half past four both Harry and Rebecca were shooting beseeching, questioning looks at Bev and Deirdre after each patient. Surely there had to be some news by now? Rebecca's face felt tight from having to smile at patients, and her neck was stiff and aching.

Finally, at six, with four patients still left to see, Deirdre reported quietly, 'Her mother rang. Grace delivered half an hour ago. A boy. She's named him James Kent after her father—she and Marcus had already agreed on that, apparently—and he'll be cremated privately over the weekend. Marcus has been told. She doesn't want flowers, but people can make a donation to charity in the baby's name. And she'd like you to drop in and see her after you finish, Rebecca. She's feeling that she gave you short shrift today.'

'Oh, for heaven's sake!' Her throat tightened. 'As if I'm thinking about something like that!'

'We can go together, Rebecca,' Harry said. 'I have a patient I'd like to see.'

He touched her lightly and deliberately on the arm, and as always her awareness of him flamed through her at once. She longed just to lean against him, bury her face in his neck and drink in the subtle scent of his warm skin... She didn't do it, of course.

A second later he turned to Bev and Deirdre. 'As soon as the waiting-room's empty, you two should go. It's late, and you've got your families. We'll tidy and lock up.' Even the way he used the word 'we' did something to Rebecca's insides.

It was after six-thirty by the time they left, each taking their own car. They met up just outside the main entrance, but would soon split up again as Harry was heading to one of the two surgical wards. Then, in the foyer, they both saw Marcus stride out of the lift, and he almost bumped into them, before realising who they were.

Rebecca was hugely relieved to see him. Surely the loss of their child would have brought him and Grace together! What Grace had said about ending their marriage today had been emotion and hysteria, not something real and thought-out. If he was just coming from her room now...

'How is she?' she asked him at once.

But the obstetrician's pale, handsomely chiselled face was haggard and his voice hoarse as he replied, 'She won't see me. She says I never wanted the baby in the first place and, my God, she's right... She's right...'

He lurched away from them and almost crashed into the automatic doors, moving so fast he hadn't given them time to part.

'Hell!' Harry rasped, then searched Rebecca's face, his dark eyes narrowed. They were standing very close, as if seeking support from each other. 'Did you know about this?'

'We all knew something was wrong,' she said helplessly. 'I didn't know it was this. Grace said today that her marriage was over. I hoped it was just her agony over losing the baby, that she was getting things out of proportion, or— Oh, Harry!'

She pressed her face into her hands, then felt his fingers come to rest lightly on her shoulders and chafe them. 'Meet you back here?' he suggested. 'I'd like to see Grace, too, but she doesn't need crowds today. Tell me how she is.'

'OK.'

Rebecca didn't spend long with Grace. She had been moved down to the gynae ward and had eaten an evening meal. Her mother, Mrs Kent, was currently doing the same down in the hospital cafeteria. Now Grace looked exhausted, and she admitted, 'They've given me something to help me sleep. I—I hope it kicks in soon.'

'Yes, you need to rest.'

'Mum's been so good...'

She didn't mention Marcus, and Rebecca didn't ask. Now wasn't the time. 'If there's anything at all I can do,' she said, and that was the closest she could get to what really mattered. 'I mean that, Grace, and I know it goes for Dad, Harry, everyone.'

'I know.' Grace nodded. 'Thanks. But I'm fine. It…wasn't a hard delivery, and Julius said there should be no complications of any kind. I'll be back at work on Monday.'

'Grace—'

'Please. Don't argue. I *need* to, Rebecca!'

Harry and Rebecca arrived back in the main hospital foyer within a minute of each other, and it felt so good just to see him that Rebecca let her feelings show openly on her face. He, too, wasn't attempting to hide what he felt after the draining emotions of the day. His gaze washed over her, searching and heated, and as soon as they were standing together he touched her, reaching out to tangle his fingers lightly in hers. She could feel the heat of her awareness flooding up her arm.

'OK?'

'Course not!'

'No. No, I know…' Their fingers twined together more tightly and she felt the warmth of his arm against hers.

'Harry, Dad's away… I don't want to spend the weekend alone.' As soon as the words were out, she knew how they must have sounded, and added quickly, 'I'm sorry. I didn't mean… That is, just if you'd like dinner, or—'

'My God, Rebecca,' he cut in, his voice husky and low. 'Don't apologise! If you *did* mean it, there's nothing I'd like better!'

'Oh…good.' She nodded shakily, then just stood there, still gripping his fingers, staring at his chest and not knowing what else to say.

'So… Do you want to eat out, or shall we get take-away?' he asked gently at last.

'Oh…out,' she answered at once. Thank goodness he only seemed to be thinking about dinner! 'I think I need some…some space, or something.'

His grip tightened on her hand. 'Of course. We both do. Let's take my car.'

'Fine.' It didn't seem important.

'We'll pick up yours…' he waved vaguely '…whenever. It's in the doctors' car park, isn't it?'

'Mmm.' She had no desire to argue. 'Grace says she'll be back at work on Monday,' she told Harry as they left the building.

He didn't seem surprised. 'She's tough, Grace, beyond that soft, maternal exterior.'

'*That's* what you think it is? *Toughness?*'

'Yes,' he retorted. 'She'll be so tough about this she'll probably end up breaking into a million pieces, but if you're suggesting that us making her take…what? A week off? Two? If you think that will stop it from happening, then I doubt it. Whatever this thing is between her and Marcus, and about him not wanting the child, it's very big and very deep, and losing the baby is either going to get them through it and back together, stronger than before, or break them permanently apart.'

'Either way, I'm not sure that we can do anything, except what Grace says she wants. I'm also not sure that talking and agonising over it is going to do anything for her, or for us. Probably the reverse, in fact.'

'You know everything, don't you, Harry?' she said with biting sarcasm. Why was she angry? Probably because she sensed strongly that he was right.

He turned on her. 'Hey! Are we going to spend the whole weekend fighting?'

The looming threat of his strong body failed to cow her. 'We fight a lot, Harry, in case you hadn't noticed,' she retorted, while her nipples hardened treacherously as she caught his scent and warmth in her nostrils.

'Oh, I'd noticed,' he drawled dangerously. 'Believe me! But I wondered if perhaps we were getting past that now. Don't you think we both need to change our perspectives a little?'

'No.' She decided to brazen it out.

Useless, of course. He'd started running his palms lightly

up her arms and even as she contradicted him she was swaying towards him in a movement of complete betrayal.

He gave a lazy grin. 'In that case, I have to presume that you like a little conflict in a relationship.'

'Uh…' Now his hands had grown bolder and he was stroking her upper arms so that, with increasing frequency, his thumbs began to brush against her breasts.

'Well, OK, Rebecca, that's fine with me. Conflict—the right kind—makes heat, and there's definitely nothing wrong with heat, is there?'

'No…' The word got caught in her throat.

He was playing with her—he knew exactly what she was thinking and feeling—and she didn't care. Let him! Just let him, as long as it meant he still held her like this, still kissed her like this…because he was kissing her now, right here in the doctors' car park, in the lee of the building, beside his car.

First, with his strong hands coming lightly to rest on her shoulders, he kissed her neck with darting, nibbling, teasing touches of his lips. Next his cheek brushed her face, he made a small sound of need deep in his throat and his mouth moved across her face to meet what he was looking for—her lips, which he began to taste and part and thrust between with a lazy, teasing tongue.

She sighed shakily and gave in to her own longing to put her arms around his neck, feel the strength of his shoulders and the thick softness of his dark hair, and it was only then that one phrase in what he had said a few moments ago came back to her with fresh significance.

'Spend the whole weekend'? So he hadn't just meant dinner, after all…

CHAPTER NINE

NEITHER Harry nor Rebecca was in any hurry. They didn't need to say so, but they both knew.

First, he drove her home to feed Muffin, then they headed out towards Watson's Bay and picked up take-away fish and chips with coleslaw, a bottle of chilled white wine, and—romantic, this—a packet of clear plastic disposable cups. Their mutual need to seek air and perspective and distance was instinctive.

It was a gorgeous evening after last week's rain, and it felt good to eat their meal on a well-placed bench overlooking the cliffs of South Head, then ramble along the cliff-top path, looking out across the Tasman Sea towards New Zealand.

Sometimes they talked, but mostly silence felt easier…safer. Rebecca was full of the knowledge that they were going to spend the weekend together. It felt far more natural than saying goodnight at some arbitrary point later in the evening, and tonight she wanted to contemplate neither the past in their relationship, with its hostility and frightening strength of attraction, nor the unknown of the future.

After half an hour of walking, they stopped back at their original bench and he poured more wine and they watched the darkening heave of the ocean once more. An oil tanker powered its silent way between the square-cut cliffs of the heads, and Harry voiced her own thought when he said, 'I can never see a ship without wondering where it's come from or where it's going.'

She confessed, 'I considered the Navy at one stage—as a doctor, I mean.'

'That can be quite a career. But you changed your mind. Why?'

'Um...' She laughed. 'Silly reason. I didn't want to spoil the dream by finding out what the reality was like. I didn't want to risk *not* wondering where ships were coming from.'

'Not silly at all,' he answered. 'Have to be careful with our dreams sometimes, pick the ones we're going to act on and the ones we're going to keep. Like my old collection of shells in a way. I still have them, wrapped up in tissue paper in a box in the top of my wardrobe. I never do anything with them, but I like to know they're there. Something like that...'

'It wasn't the only reason,' she said quickly. Despite what he'd said about the shells, which rang true, she wanted him to know that at heart she made important decisions about her life on a less whimsical basis.

'I thought about what that life would involve,' she went on. 'Frequently uprooting and being away from home, the potential for real danger, and I decided it might demand more sacrifice than I could give. I didn't want to risk... It sounds like I'm very afraid of risk, doesn't it? I didn't want to risk feeling that I couldn't marry or have children, and I didn't want to feel that if marriage and children did come they'd come at a huge sacrifice and involve terrible choices and compromises.'

'You really thought it through. This was when you were...?'

'Eighteen,' she supplied.

'I doubt that I was thinking with that degree of maturity about my future at eighteen.'

'Losing my mother at fifteen forced me to grow up more quickly perhaps,' she said, 'Sorry, this is getting very serious, isn't it?' Then she bit her lip at the unintended double meaning. She hadn't meant their relationship.

To her relief, he just said lightly, 'It's the stars. It's very difficult to be shallow and trivial when the stars are listening to what you say.'

She laughed. 'Funny how you say these quirky things that I've never thought of before, and I suddenly find they're true.'

'Call it a gift,' he teased.

'I will.' She looked at him and saw how intently he was watching her, taking in what she'd said.

'Your mother's death had a huge impact on you, didn't it? You've told me that.'

'Not a negative one, Harry, in the end.'

'No?'

'Because it taught me that caring and feeling are the most important things. The *only* things. Whatever or whoever it is you care for. I mean, what's the point of having something in your life if it *doesn't* make you hurt when you lose it? You have to face up to life as if it's a huge storm and bare your face to it and say here I am. Give me all you've got, the good and the bad...' She trailed off. It suddenly occurred to her that she was talking about Harry. 'You *have* to,' she finished, facing up to what that meant.

They'd touched frequently since those moments in the doctors' car park. He'd taken her hand as they'd climbed a rock, or brushed his fingers across her shoulders or her hip, weaving a web of shared desire around both of them.

But they hadn't kissed. He was ready to make that complete now, and so was she. It was all the more powerful for having been delayed.

'Time, Rebecca,' he murmured.

'Time?'

'Yes, because I can't stand it any longer. I have to taste you.' And his mouth was hungry on hers before he'd even finished the words.

It was like being enveloped in a warm mist. His arms, wrapped around her, were impossibly tender and impossibly strong at the same time, and his kiss was both demanding and giving in equal measure. Her response was as hungry and hon-

est as his, and he seemed to glory in knowing the strength of
what he did to her.

'Love it, love the way you're like this,' he said huskily.
'Such passion and such completeness.' He broke off for a moment and laughed. 'You have no idea how good it is for a
man to know that when he kisses a woman she's not thinking
about what it might be doing to her hair.'

'Her *hair*?' She reached up and touched the wildly curling
mass, which she'd long ago given up on controlling successfully. The clip which had fastened it during the day was sitting
somewhere at the bottom of her bag.

'You'd be surprised, Rebecca,' he drawled, reaching up to
caress her hand then coaxing it away so that he had her hair
to himself.

'Sounds like something—*someone*—I don't want to know
about!' she told him.

'You don't and you won't and you needn't. She was months
ago, and you're…in a class of your own. I'm tempted to think
they broke the mould…'

His mouth was on hers again, more urgent this time, draw-
ing even more from her so that several minutes later she was
hardly aware of who had said what, only that they were going
to his place and both of them knew exactly why.

For her, at the ripe old age of twenty-seven, it was the first
time, and she didn't know how to tell him so. The glaring fact
of it consumed her in the car and she wondered if he'd want
reasons, explanations—*excuses*? There *were* those, of course.

There was her mother's death, which had taken up so much
of her emotional energy for years afterwards as she'd focused
on Dad's and Simon's needs, and which had taught her,
through the depth of her father's grief, more than most young
women in their late teens understood about what real love
meant.

There was her own passionate nature, too, which at times
she'd curbed quite consciously. She'd known that sleeping

with a man would push her over that invisible, vital brink between involvement and love, and since the near-disaster with Matt, who'd boasted of his conquest just a little too soon, she hadn't met a man she'd wanted to feel like that for.

Until Harry.

It was frightening to know that she was able to let go of that protective barrier at last, and it wasn't a rational decision either. Somehow, with Harry, need was about to overcome anything else, and as she felt the storm of her own surrender to him growing inexorably closer she could only trust that if it felt like this then it had to be right.

They were inside his house before she found a way to say it, and even then it was so unlike her, so tentative and ambiguous, that a less perceptive man might not have understood. Facing him and looking up into his dark eyes, she simply said, 'Harry, help me…with this, won't you?'

Rebecca saw the flare of surprise and comprehension in his face, but he didn't say anything at first, just nodded slowly. Then, just as slowly, he pulled her into his arms and laid her head on his shoulder.

'I will,' he whispered, 'As long as you help me. Talk to me, OK, if *any* of it feels wrong.'

There was no going back on his part after those words. Harry knew that, as he took Rebecca's hand and led her up the stairs at his side.

Would I have gone back, though, said no to this, if somehow I'd known…or guessed…before? he wondered.

Perhaps it shouldn't even have been a question, but somehow it was. There was Marsh hovering somewhere in the background. His senior partner, whom he so respected. He felt his responsibility to father and daughter trebled now, and realised as they reached his bedroom that in this moment he could well be more terrified than she was…

No… Flicking his glance to her face to study it quickly, he discovered that she wasn't frightened now at all, and oddly this at once made everything all right. *Better* than all right. *Wonderful!*

Exultant desire sizzled within him. She trusts me. She *trusts* me enough to embark on a journey like this without fear...

He hadn't turned on the light, Rebecca realised. The corridor was lit up, and the pale, simple curtains of the tall, sashed window opposite the bed were open. Immediately that felt right. The night at South Head had been like a friend, and more powerful than the wine in making things smooth between them. Now it felt like the night was seeping into the room to once again contribute its benign presence—a presence which day-bright electricity would have brashly chased away.

He kissed her now, and it was like the opening act of a play, a seamless part of what was to follow. She was trembling, ready for this, not frightened any more but still aware of the sheer *size* of such a milestone in her life after so long. Then suddenly, under the tender onslaught of his lips, all this momentousness faded and fell away and became unimportant, and all that counted was what her body felt and wanted and understood.

She hardly knew when he began to unfasten her blouse, only that all at once its fine cotton fell from her shoulders with a cool caress and his bare arms had closed around her back in a heated, wonderful imprisonment. She could feel her breasts in their pale blue satin cups pressing against his dark blue shirt, and was wantonly hungry to experience the raw graze of his chest hair against her hardened nipples.

Impatiently, she fumbled for his shirt buttons but, fumbling or not, she wouldn't let him help her when he tried to, so instead he took on another task—unclipping her bra at the back.

Seconds later skin touched skin, and it pushed her physical need onto another even deeper and more powerful level so that they were both racing to shed the rest of their clothes.

His bed...

He turned from her to wrench the covers back, then wrapped his arms round her tenderly once again, one hand splayed across her back and the other tracing the firm, soft curves of her bottom. Now he was lifting her, and a moment later he'd laid her on the pale striped sheets, his eyes running over her in the dim light, their dark depths filled with smouldering fire.

He knelt beside her, the distant light from the corridor sculpting his chest and shoulders with dark shadow that emphasised his muscles. His hand came out and stroked her face, then wandered down to reach and lightly cup her swollen breasts, and she arched and shuddered convulsively in anticipation of something she didn't yet even understand.

'It's not too late to stop,' he said softly. 'You know that, don't you? If you want to, at any point, it won't be too late.'

'That's not what I've always heard about how it is for a man,' she whispered with a degree of irony in her tone.

'No? Well, don't underestimate my self-control.'

'I won't…'

'Speaking of which, excuse me for a moment.'

He disappeared, and she heard him in the adjoining bathroom, sliding open the front of a cabinet. He was back within seconds. 'Don't underestimate my sense of responsibility either,' he drawled, as he placed a small blue packet on the bedside table.

After this, Rebecca didn't do much estimating—much *thinking*, in fact—for quite a long time. She was caught up in a maelstrom of touch and taste and inner, pulsing sensation. There was just one moment of pain, so blurred with the swelling of her desire that she was scarcely aware of it, and then they both rushed headlong towards a climax which left her aching and shaken and awestruck so that she had to cling to him as if to a life-raft.

They lay like this for several minutes, and as her own churning aftermath subsided she became aware that he was as breathless and overcome as she was. When he spoke, his voice was a husky creak. '*Now* it's too late to stop, OK?'

She laughed, and he kissed her lazily. Minutes later they were both asleep, still entwined tightly together.

Rebecca didn't awaken until morning, and even then it wasn't the bright light of late spring that woke her but the subtle eroticism of Harry's touch—fingers moving like paintbrushes to make intricate patterns of sensation all over her skin as he caressed hip and stomach and shoulder and breast.

An instant pulse of need deep in her centre had her eyes flaring open in shock.

He was watching her. 'I didn't wake you, did I?'

His tone made it clear that he was totally unrepentant if he had.

'What do you want me to say?' she asked lazily.

'I want you to say, "Yes, but please wake me up more,"' he suggested, without batting an eyelid.

'Bad luck,' she teased back. 'I'm already wide, *wide* awake.'

'Call me an opportunist, then,' he mumbled, and rolled her into his arms.

Muffin got his breakfast rather late that morning, during a flying visit back to Centennial Park. 'Don't complain, Kitty-pie,' Rebecca told him. 'I haven't had mine yet either!'

That was next on the agenda. Harry had gone to pick up croissants and the newspaper, and to keep Muffin company they breakfasted in the big kitchen at Rebecca's.

'What do you have on this weekend?' Harry asked when they'd finished the relaxed meal.

'You mean apart from covering the practice?'

They were both doing that, but weren't anticipating being called out. There were no babies due at the moment, and obstetric work accounted for the bulk of the practice's out-of-hours calls. Emergencies went to the hospital, and phone consults—usually about a feverish or asthmatic child, or an elderly patient at Hazel Cleary Lodge—were generally brief.

'Yes,' Harry answered her. 'Please don't say you've got dates and parties and barbecues all weekend!'

As usual, she liked his frankness, and grinned at it. Then she thought a little guiltily of David, whom she'd promised to contact during the week and hadn't.

'Nothing on,' she told Harry, understanding only now just how much phoning David originally had actually been all about Harry, and her fear of arriving at exactly the point she was at now—love. Physically sating, emotionally dizzying, overpowering love.

Right at this moment, not willing to think beyond this weekend, this room, this instant, she could only wonder what she'd been so afraid of.

'How about you?' she added softly, with a caress in her voice.

'Busy,' he answered. 'But if you'll come too, we'll have a great weekend.'

They did. Saturday was a day meant for laziness and love. The deep blue Australian sky held white fluffy clouds that coasted through it on a fresh, cool breeze from the south-west. They walked in the park and had a light snack instead of lunch as they'd breakfasted so late, then went back to his place, where the inevitable happened. Slower, this time. More exploratory. With talking and laughing in between.

Showering together afterwards was a sensuous and slippery and tantalising experience, and if Harry hadn't had two tickets for Jade Staley's pre-Christmas ice-skating show at eight o'clock, who knew what it might have led to?

'Do you often take women to suburban ice shows, featuring large groups of schoolchildren who can't skate very well?' she whispered in his ear as they sat down in the uncomfortable plastic seats and felt the chill of the rink creeping up to them.

The first group of skaters was already milling awkwardly

around the ice, as if half of them had forgotten where they were supposed to start.

'Sorry… Was it a bad idea?' He grimaced, looking alarmed. 'Jade gave me the tickets, and I know how hard she works at her sport, so—'

'Joke, Harry. Joke,' she soothed. 'Relax! It's going to be great fun. I have a good excuse to do something I wouldn't normally do, and you've got me quite interested in Jade.'

And in the end it was a great evening. The show's organisers had had the good sense to intersperse stumbling groups of tots and rocky soloists with the stars at the rink, including professional coaches such as Stephen Carr and Danielle McGrath, who'd been to three Winter Olympic Games as amateurs and had won the Australian pairs title more times than anyone could count. This meant that the evening was a charming blend of dazzling display and poignant falls.

During the latter moments, Rebecca unashamedly watched the parents, who sat on the edges of their seats in fear or clapped their hands and smiled with radiant love and pride. Her heart twisted several times as she did this, thinking of Grace, who'd had her imminent motherhood so painfully thwarted. With her marriage itself in doubt, when would she get another chance?

Harry, meanwhile, wasn't watching the skaters or the parents. He was watching Rebecca. He loved the way her face was so alive with interest and involvement, loved her readiness to enter into the spirit of the event.

Then came twelve-year-old Jade in a glittering costume, to scissor and whirl her way across the ice to the rhythm of dramatic classical music. Although her skating did not yet have the maturity of some of the older stars, there was a quality to it which both Harry and Rebecca recognised at once, and when her music died away and the applause rang out Harry whispered smugly, 'I knew she'd be good. She worked so hard on getting that ankle strong and fit again, and it didn't let her down, did it? I didn't see any wobbles on her landings.'

There was a crush when the show ended. Everyone wanted to congratulate friends or siblings or children, so Rebecca and Harry didn't attempt to find Jade and speak to her. It was getting late now, and they were happy—more than happy—to slip away on their own.

Back to his place. Again, it didn't even need to be said, and the growing familiarity of each other's bodies sparked rapture twice before sleep came.

Awakening on Sunday, however, with Harry still stretched out beside her, his breathing heavy and his strong, tanned arms flung up on the pillow, Rebecca already felt as if paradise was ending today. Yesterday had been so perfect, suspended in a world apart from reality. Now…

The hours ahead felt too short. Dad would be back late this afternoon. Her car was still sitting forlornly in the doctors' car park at Southshore. Grace would probably be discharged to-day. Would she go straight to her mother's? Dad didn't know about the loss of the baby yet. Rebecca hadn't wanted to spoil his weekend by phoning him with the news when there was nothing at all he could have done.

But would Grace really be physically and emotionally fit to return to work tomorrow?

It all went round and round in her head, and she only now understood how seductively easy it had been to mask all this by capitulating at last to what she'd felt for Harry for so many weeks. Deceptively convenient. But what would happen next?

As Harry slept on, she watched him almost greedily, as if laying these moments away in store—a reserve that might be all too necessary some time soon in the future.

He stirred at last, and as soon as she saw his face she knew that he, too, was aware of the looming end of their idyll.

First, though, he'd promised to go and see Shane McNeill race, his first competition—more of a test really as it was only a small event on the cycling calendar—since the injury to his knee. Somehow, though, Rebecca couldn't drum up the same enthusiasm for this that she'd had for Jade's show last night. Was it only that skating was prettier?

They breakfasted quickly, without yesterday's sense that time didn't matter. Shane had two races, apparently, and had asked that Harry be there for both of them. Unfortunately, they were at opposite ends of the programme of events, and before driving out to the outdoor velodrome at Tempe they had to go and give Muffin his breakfast again.

Poor little puss had probably been a bit lonely this weekend, though he'd had all the creature comforts a cat could need— a soft, warm bed, food and drink and a clean litter tray. They could, of course, have kept him company by staying at Rebecca's, but Harry hadn't suggested it and somehow neither had she.

She had been practical enough to bring a change of clothes back to Harry's last night, however—just the pink T-shirt and denim jeans he'd seen her in before.

As they set off he teased her. 'Didn't I once mention that I liked you in pink?'

In the end, Rebecca enjoyed the cycling more than she'd thought she would, at least at first. The first event was a scratch race, five kilometres long, mainly designed as a warm-up, with about twenty riders competing to be first across the line after their fifteen laps. Shane won it easily and his knee felt good, but he wanted Harry to give the knee a thorough going-over before tackling his kilometre sprint which was still to come. This was the event that was his strongest.

There wasn't much of a crowd at the event. Harry and Rebecca had been able to sit where they wanted and, after catching Shane's first race, had naturally met up with Lisa, who was standing anxiously as close to the front barrier as she could get. That wasn't very close these days as her pregnant stomach seemed to jut vastly.

I've seen her quite recently, Rebecca thought as they first caught sight of Lisa. Now, when had it been? She had to struggle to remember back across her timeless sojourn in paradise.

Then it hit her. Friday. Just two days ago. It was hearing Lisa, talking about being kicked to pieces, which had triggered Grace's realisation that she hadn't felt her own baby move for some time.

Now, as the two women stood in one of the athletes' dressing-rooms upstairs at the back of the grandstand, watching Harry bending and stretching and pressing and pulling Shane's taped and muscle-knotted leg, Rebecca told Lisa quietly, 'There's some bad news you ought to know, I'm afraid, Lisa. Dr Gaines lost her baby on Friday afternoon.'

'Oh, *no*!' Lisa instinctively clasped her hands over her own stomach. 'How?'

'He'd died *in utero*.' She didn't want to frighten Lisa by going into too much detail. 'There was nothing anyone could have done. She went to Southshore and they induced labour. Physically Grace is doing fine.'

'She— Presumably she'll take some time off?'

'Well, she says not.' Rebecca didn't mention that Grace had also left her husband. No one beyond the staff at the practice needed to know that. 'But we'll see how things go. If she does take your next appointment, I know you'll be sensitive about how hard this is for her.'

'Yes... Oh, heavens, yes!' Lisa's eyes had filled with tears. 'We were both due on Christmas Day. Shane, did you hear?'

He nodded slowly. 'Rough! Really rough! Makes you realise... One way or another, as soon as you even decide to *try* for a baby, your life is never the same again.'

'Looks great, Shane,' Harry said quietly. 'No sign at all of the kneecap pulling sideways as it was before. It feels as firm as the other one now. Leave the tape off it this time. Just to make sure, though, we'll check it again after the next race, and you'll obviously let me know if anything feels wrong.'

But in the end Harry didn't check it after the next race. Still looking subdued and sad after hearing the news about Grace, Lisa winced and flinched suddenly a few minutes later, then told her baby, 'Hey, are you kicking a football in there?'

A flood of warm, clear fluid gushed onto the floor before she'd even finished the words. All four of them knew what it meant.

'I shouldn't wait, should I?' Lisa said. 'I should go to hospital because if labour doesn't start on its own they'll have to induce me.'

'Yes,' Rebecca said. 'Because the uterus is no longer a sterile environment. Your baby's vulnerable to infection from outside now.'

Shane looked a question at his wife, and she understood at once. 'Stay for the race,' she told him. 'I don't expect things will go that fast. You'll get there in time. Who'll deliver me now, Dr Irwin?'

'I can, if you'd like. Or a hospital-based doctor or midwife. It's really your choice.'

'I'd like you, if that's all right. You know…a familiar face. I—I don't feel quite ready for this. I wasn't expecting it for five weeks, and after what you told me about poor Dr Gaines, I'm…*scared*.' Her voice caught. 'The baby's still premature.'

Shane said nothing. He was pulling the tough athletic support tape from his leg. It came away with a loud ripping noise.

'Um, as far as getting there—' Lisa said, then her husband cut in abruptly.

'Stuff the race,' he said. 'It doesn't matter. It's not the Nationals, and even if it were—I want to be with *you*, Lisa,' he finished gruffly.

She burst into tears. 'I love you!' she said, then added forcefully, 'But, Shane McNeill, if you think I'd let you miss the

Nationals this year, when it's so important, then you don't know me very well!'

'A convenient way to return you to your car,' Harry said some time later as they pulled up once more in the doctors' car park. Shane and Lisa had taken their own vehicle.

'Yes, it was. Thanks, Harry,' Rebecca answered him, not remotely ready to say goodbye.

'Want me to hang around?'

'No, don't bother. I'll stay until she's checked in and see how everything is going. If it looks like it's moving fast I won't bother to go home, and if it's not moving at all I'll need to talk to her and Shane about the pros and cons of induction. Either way…'

Either way the weekend was over, and they both knew it.

'See you tomorrow, then,' Harry said, aware that his casual tone wasn't quite genuine.

'Yes… Bye,' she answered briefly, and the word was punctuated by the metallic *thunk* of his passenger-side door closing.

He watched her, wondering if she'd turn round, but she didn't, though in the last few seconds before she disappeared through a side entrance he was actually *willing* it. Turn, Rebecca. Turn! *Wave*, for God's sake! No, for *my* sake. Your body from behind is fabulous, and just to look at it is stirring me to the point of pain, but it's your face I want to see. Your smile, with a promise in it. Turn and smile for me, *please*!

But the door that led to the lifts had shut behind her now and, despite his desperate attempts at telepathy, she hadn't looked back once. He sat there for some minutes more, trying to work out why it mattered so much.

Because of Marsh, he finally decided. Because of what he'd known all along about the complex double triangle of father-daughter-lover and senior partner-junior partner-new recruit. He and Rebecca had just spent a weekend together which had been about as close to perfect as real life could get, and the natural thing to do would be to pick up straight from where they'd left off as soon as it was decently possible to do so, but Rebecca was living under her father's roof so how could he possibly turn up there and say to Marshall, 'Excuse me, I've come to pick up your daughter and take her home to bed!'

He couldn't, of course. Not like that!

No doubt, however, the thing could be managed in a clandestine fashion—hurried sexual skirmishings in the evenings before she hastily got herself dressed again so she could be home at a decent hour.

Or could she, in fact, spend the night with him quite openly? Marsh was a realistic, modern, sensible man, and Rebecca was twenty-seven years old.

I could do it, Harry decided, if he was *just* my lover's father. I could do it if she was *just* our new practice partner.

It was their dual roles that created the problem, and he could feel this fact forcing the pace of their relationship—of his feelings—in a way that seemed to contain all the danger he'd feared from the moment he'd set eyes on her.

There was simply no room for mistakes in what happened between himself and Rebecca from now on. There never had been room, and with his added weight of experience and age he knew that he had to be the one to dictate the pace and make the decisions. The fact of her virginity—her *recent* virginity, he amended wryly to himself—only added another ingredient to the already sizzling cocktail.

With a roiling wash of self-doubt, he wondered if he had what it would take to make everyone happy. How would they all find themselves six months from now? His partnership with Marsh in the Irwin practice soured because he'd hurt Rebecca and her father couldn't forgive it? Himself the heartbroken also-ran, while Rebecca was wildly in love with some new man who was reaping all the benefits of her newly unleashed sensuality?

Not surprisingly, neither of the above appealed to him in the slightest.

I shouldn't have slept with her this weekend, he decided in frustration at last. It had felt so right… It had been right in so many ways. But we should have held back, and I was the only one who could have put the brakes on.

Angry at his lack of long-term vision, even while knowing how easy it was to be wise *after* the event, Harry at last drove home.

CHAPTER TEN

KNOWING that Lisa McNeill would still be getting herself settled while Shane went over admission details, Rebecca first went to the gynae floor to see if she could find out any news about Grace. She and Harry had talked about visiting yesterday, but had decided against it.

On Friday Grace had seemed determined on privacy and on holding herself together. She had wanted her mother, and that was all. Now, on asking at the nurses' station, Rebecca wasn't surprised to learn that Dr Gaines had been discharged this morning at her own request.

'There was no reason why not,' the ward sister explained quietly. 'Medically it was an easy delivery, and emotionally she didn't want to stay here a second longer than she needed to. Well, I don't really need to explain…'

'No,' Rebecca agreed. 'So, did she go home with—?'

'Her mother,' Gillian Fielding said.

Rebecca nodded again, and their eyes met briefly. Sister Fielding would know Marcus, of course, as he had surgical patients here all the time. Both women knew that more was going on than just the loss of the baby, devastating though that was. Neither of them had the slightest desire to hurt Grace with gossip or conjecture.

'I have the number at her mother's.' That was all Rebecca said. 'I expect my father will phone her tonight.'

Up on Maternity, things were much more cheerful. Lisa's contractions had started in the car and were coming steadily about ten minutes apart. The cervix was about seventy per cent effaced and one centimetre dilated on manual examination, and Lisa was feeling energetic and confident and well able to walk around the corridor to help speed things up. She and Shane had also been shown the special premmie equipment and facilities, and had been told what to expect. These days, a baby coming five weeks early was almost always at low risk for prematurity-related problems.

There was no need for Rebecca to stay at this stage.

'I'll be back once things really hot up,' she promised, and drove home to find Dad there, unpacking his suitcase.

He had driven himself to the airport on Friday morning and had left his car in the long-stay car park over the weekend.

'Really nice,' he reported on his two-night stay. 'The wedding was charming—the whole wedding party actually looked tastefully dressed!'

'Dad! Even the bridesmaids?' Rebecca teased.

A veteran of several weddings over the past few years—usually the daughters of old friends—Dad had developed strong feelings on what he called 'peacock bridesmaids and pavlova brides'. He preferred a simpler look.

They talked about his trip for several minutes more, and then came the hard part.

'I'm afraid there's been some very bad news since you left, Dad,' she began, and felt her eyes fill with the tears she'd tricked herself into forgetting over the weekend.

Half an hour later Dad put down the phone, after speaking to Grace. 'Yes, she says she's coming in tomorrow. I didn't forbid it. She wants to keep busy, and maybe that's best—just fight her way through life until things gradually get better. You haven't seen or heard from Marcus since Friday night?'

'No. I've just come from the hospital.' She explained briefly about Lisa McNeill. 'I looked for Marcus. He didn't seem to be about. I don't know...what I would have said if he had been.'

'No,' Dad agreed. 'It's...hellish. There's really nothing we can do to help beyond what Grace actually asks for. Marriages do break down, and often it can happen over the sort of tragedy that should pull people together. It's early days. We can only hope they sort it out. But, anyway, tell me about *your* weekend.'

What did one say? Rebecca had had absolutely no practice at this at all, and to her own ears it showed. She stumbled vaguely through something about Muffin and being lazy and Harry taking her to see his skater perform, making sure that she was fumbling in her bag when she said his name so that Dad wouldn't see…whatever there was in her face to see.

She was vastly relieved when her pager went off.

'It's the hospital. It must be Lisa already. I hope there's not a problem.'

There wasn't, but things were coming along faster than usual for a first baby.

'Sorry to have to get you to turn straight round again,' a nurse said. 'It looks like it's going to be an easy delivery, but she'd like to have you here.'

'And I'd like to be there,' Rebecca said truthfully. After the loss of Grace's baby, she needed a happy ending.

'Will you eat when you get back?' Dad wanted to know.

'No, don't worry about me,' she answered quickly. 'I'll grab something somewhere.'

'Okey-doke. See you later.'

He gave her a quick peck on the cheek and she felt guilty, remorseful, deceitful.

This was all about Harry. She had spent the weekend with Harry while Dad was away. Dad didn't know about it, and she didn't know where it was going from here, and now she couldn't meet Dad's eye in case he somehow *guessed*.

Which was stupid because Dad, of all people, would be only too happy to know that she was in love.

'As long as it worked out,' Rebecca said to herself aloud as she drove back down Anzac Parade. 'That's the crunch. If it's not going to work out, then I don't want him to know anything about it at all.'

She didn't know why she was thinking like this—they'd had a fabulous weekend together, after all—except that this was the end of the nineties and relationships weren't predictable any more, and she'd given herself to Harry two days ago—that was an old-fashioned idea perhaps, *giving* yourself to a man, but all the same that was how it felt—and it made a huge difference somehow.

It would matter so much if it turned out to be just a weekend…or just a few weekends, or six months of weekends…and the more it mattered the more likely it seemed that something would go wrong.

She'd already been thinking this way when she'd left Harry in the car park an hour and a half ago. That was why she'd steeled herself very deliberately not to look back at him, holding herself so tightly that her shoulders ached. He mustn't think that she'd slept with him in order to bind him to her in some way. He mustn't think she was forcing the pace.

Lisa McNeill was caught in the thick of active labour when Rebecca reached her room, the strong contractions coming so hard on top of each other that it would be difficult to find a brief respite in which to examine her. Lisa was working hard to stay in control, but her legs were shaking now and midwife Alix Bowman only just got to her with a bowl in time as she retched and then vomited.

Shane was coaching Lisa through the contractions with almost equal energy, and it took Rebecca, who was capped and gowned now with well-washed hands, a moment to gather herself and slot in to all the activity.

'OK… This is it. This is it!' Lisa suddenly said, and her urge to push was so strong that she fought off any attempt to check her dilatation.

It didn't matter. As she pulled on her thighs and arched back on the bed, the dark, wet head was already crowning strongly, and Rebecca easily massaged back one edge of the cervix that was curled and getting in the way. Three mighty pushes was all it took to bring out the head, then the shoulders rotated easily and the whole baby slipped out, looking a good sturdy size for dates—as much as six pounds, Rebecca estimated, and already crying.

'A boy, Lisa,' she said.

Like Grace's little lost James.

'Oh!' Lisa exclaimed incoherently. 'Oh… Oh!' Shane stifled several sobs. Less than three hours ago they'd been thinking of his cycling, not this.

For the next ten minutes or so the room was very busy and noisy. Lisa hadn't torn at all, but Rebecca had the cord and placenta to deliver and examine while Lisa cradled her new baby on her chest for a few precious moments until he was taken away to be checked by a hospital paediatrician who specialised in premmie babies. This one, though, looked so robust and healthy that he seemed like a fraud.

'I wouldn't be surprised if your dates were a bit wrong,' Rebecca told Lisa. 'Or perhaps you conceived very early in your cycle.'

It was nice to have some good news to report to Dad when she got home, after stopping to eat a hamburger in the car on the way. It hadn't been a very sensible solution to dinner, and Dad understandably expressed surprise after he'd heard the brief story of the birth and quizzed her about the state of her stomach.

'But if you were only going to have that,' he pointed out, 'you could have had one at home. We have all the ingredients, and it's only six-thirty now. I haven't eaten yet myself. I was just whipping up some spaghetti.'

'Well, you know, I—I wasn't sure,' Rebecca answered, then mumbled something incoherent about having a bath. She didn't meet his eye, and her cheeks were red.

Marshall watched her go in utter astonishment. She wasn't behaving naturally at all! It didn't take him more than a few moments to conclude that it had something to do with Harry.

She had been so suspiciously off-hand when mentioning his name and that they'd been out together—even if it had only been to see one of his patients perform in a suburban show.

He'd been wondering for some weeks how she really felt about Harry—all the more so because she seemed to go to such pains to conceal it, which wasn't like her. For quite some time he'd been afraid that she didn't like Harry, which would have been awkward. Lately, he'd started to wonder if she liked Harry too much, which could very well be more awkward still. Now...

They'd spent the weekend together.

As soon as the idea struck him, he knew it was true. The knowledge winded him. It shouldn't have done, of course. He was being horribly over-protective. Harry was a caring, responsible man, and Rebecca was twenty-seven years old.

Still... Still... At times he could be almost as passionate as his daughter, and he now knew the most awful temptation to get his car over to Surry Hills, hammer on his junior partner's door, seize him by the collar, threaten violence and demand to know his intentions.

He resisted it at once...and then resisted it repeatedly all evening, while Rebecca spent an hour in the bath and another hour outside playing with Muffin, before retiring to her room at a suspiciously early hour 'to read'. Theatrical yawn. 'I'm sorry, Dad. I'm *so* tired.'

Marshall sighed aloud after she'd gone, feeling more helpless than fatherhood had made him since Joy's death twelve years ago. It was horrible! Whatever had happened during their weekend together, she didn't look as if she was feeling happy about it.

Damn Harry! If he hurts her, I'll... Or is she just confused? Oh, Rebecca! Oh, Harry!

All his instincts and urges were alarmingly primitive, and if there was, in fact, something sensible and practical and wise that he ought to be doing about all this, he was at a complete loss, right now, to know what it was.

The following day was one of the most difficult ones ever known in the practice of Irwin, Gaines, Jones and Irwin. Grace was back on board, getting through by sheer force of will. The practice dealt frequently with babies, young children and pregnant women, and it was something which Grace just had to face.

'I know you think I should have taken leave,' she said at one point to Marshall, Rebecca, Andrea and Julie in the kitchen, her tone an incongruous mixture of fierceness and apology, 'But it wouldn't have been any easier to come back after a week, or two weeks, or a month. In fact, I think it's easier *now*.'

Her body language shouted the fact that she didn't want to talk at length about what was going on in her life, and everyone could only respect that wish.

Meanwhile, Rebecca couldn't help wondering if Grace's last words applied to her own situation. Was it easier now, with Harry, when they hadn't had a chance to talk and she was so wary and scared that she could hardly meet his eye naturally? Or would it be easier in a week, or two weeks, or a month, when she would know what he thought and felt once their weekend together had receded into the past?

She hoped by then, at least, that Dad's eyes wouldn't be fixed anxiously on her the way they'd been at regular intervals through the day, while he kept looking as if he had something important to say but didn't know how to start. When he and Harry spent a good part of their lunch-break shut away together in Dad's office, she had to remind herself very sternly that they'd surely only be talking about patients or recent articles in the AMA journal, or something similarly professional, so she had not the remotest reason to wonder what was being said.

She had to remind herself even more strongly of this when Harry emerged at last, looking thoughtful and determined and—possibly just a projection of her own state—more than a little hot under the collar.

Later, meeting Dad over the kettle as they both came in search of a cup of tea, she felt so on edge that she began to say impulsively, 'Dad, if there's something you want to—' But she was interrupted by Andrea, bustling in. Cheerful and chunky and blonde, she wasn't the most perceptive person in the world at times, and was quite oblivious now to the fact that she was unwanted.

In hindsight, however, Rebecca was glad she hadn't been able to complete her sentence. She didn't want Dad to guess just how much Harry was tormenting her.

Tuesday, at Southshore, was in many ways an easier day. She reported to Julius Marr that Grace seemed to be handling the return to work quite well, although Marcus's name had not been mentioned and she was still staying at her mother's.

The tall, loose-limbed GP shook his head. 'If I knew Marcus any better, maybe I'd try to talk to him, but as it is…'

'I know,' Rebecca agreed. 'That's how we feel, too—that there ought to be a way we can help, by getting one of them at least to talk it through. But Grace doesn't want to, and we hardly know Marcus.'

'Which is odd, that last thing,' Julius mused, lifting his jutting chin and looking into the middle distance. 'Because there are people I've seen a lot less of than Marcus Gaines that I'd happily say I knew reasonably well.'

'Perhaps that's part of the problem,' Rebecca answered. 'He's so reserved, and she just…*can't* talk at the moment, I don't think. They've got no meeting point. But if they can find one… If they really love each other…'

'That's the crunch, isn't it?' Julius agreed. 'If they really love each other.'

'And that's something we don't know.'

So Grace was still in her thoughts at Southshore, but at least she didn't have to confront Harry. She had hoped so much that he would phone last night, but he hadn't, and because she was conscious of waiting for a call for two hours—while carefully pretending to Dad not to be doing any such thing—she was very glad today that she was going out with David Shannon and a group of doctors from his hospital tonight.

'Just a casual, friendly meal' he'd called it, making it sound safe from anyone's perspective, and it turned out to be exactly that.

She learned when she got home from the evening at ten that this time Harry *had* phoned. Dad was very vague about it, though. Annoyingly so.

'He said it wasn't important. I told him— Well, that you'd gone out. Did you have a good time?'

'Yes, lovely. Although David is perhaps…' She hesitated.

'Not Dr Right?' Dad filled in helpfully.

Since when had he thought of her male friends in such terms?

'I was going to say,' she clarified severely, 'that he perhaps wasn't the most *interesting* person I'd ever met, actually!'

'Oh. Right. Sorry,' Dad mumbled awkwardly, then went off in rather a hurry, calling the kitten, leaving Rebecca frustrated and at a loss.

Harry didn't phone again all week so she didn't see him again until Friday. And now we're at work so it scarcely counts, she said to herself miserably. Is he just going to let it all slide? How *can* he? Have I been a fool? We seemed to need each other, to understand each other, so completely last weekend. Surely it wasn't just because of how we felt about Grace? And surely he wasn't deliberately using me? Could he be the kind of man who loses interest in a woman as soon as he's slept with her? It sounds so ugly, just like Matt would have been… Oh, why did I let this happen?

As if I could have done anything else. It sneaked up on me. I didn't *decide* to love him.

Once more the day seemed long. They didn't finish until twenty to seven so Bev and Deirdre had already left when the last three patients were ushered out.

There was one person still left in the waiting-room, however. Marcus Gaines.

Rebecca was the first to see him, and she felt a huge surge of hope for Grace as he rose from where he'd been sitting and greeted her briefly. He'd aged by years in the past week, it seemed, and again this gave her cause for further hope. If he was suffering like this then that had to give him a starting point with Grace, if Grace could only see it…

Here Grace was. 'I'll see you next week, then, Mr Massey,' she said brightly. 'You'll ring and make a follow-up appointment on Monday?'

'Right-oh,' answered the man in his sixties as he opened the front door.

Grace put his file on the front desk, and only then did she turn and see Marcus. Her face went white and she froze.

'Grace!' Marcus's voice was hoarse with strain and desperation.

'What are you doing here?'

'You *know*! I've been ringing all week and you won't come to the phone. I didn't want to have this out in front of your mother or I would have gone there. We *have* to talk!'

'No, Marcus. I can't. I'm…sorry. I just *can't*!' Grace answered, each word sounding as if she had to bite down on a knife blade to say it.

She closed her fist tightly over her car keys, wrenched open the front door and fled. Marcus's strong shoulders crumpled and he buried his face in his hands.

'This is hell,' he rasped, lifting his head again. 'I love her. And I *know* she loves me. I can't lose her! But if she won't speak to me… *What am I going to do?*'

'Give her time, Marcus,' Harry said huskily, stepping into the waiting room. He was on his own. He must have heard Grace and Marcus and had ushered his final patient quietly out the side door which was only rarely used. 'You just have to give her time,' he repeated.

Marcus nodded slowly. 'It looks as if I have little choice,' he answered, his handsome face stiff. 'Though it goes against the grain. I didn't give her much time before I proposed. Four weeks. It just seemed so obvious to me that we were meant to be together. She was—is—everything I wanted in a woman. In a wife. And now… I've ruined it all, and if time is what she wants, then, yes, I'll find the right way to give it to her— as much as she needs. What else can I do?'

He was talking to himself more than to Rebecca or Harry.

'Marcus…' Harry began, but it was too late. The obstetrician had left as abruptly as his wife.

'Call him back,' Rebecca suggested. 'He can't have gone far.'

'No…' Harry shook his head. 'I don't know what I was going to say, anyway.'

'I think what you did say was right,' Rebecca told him quietly.

'You think so? Pretty trite advice. Time…'

'Things are sometimes trite because they're true,' she pointed out. 'It's obvious that she needs time. Maybe it's not *all* she needs, but I get the impression that the very *last* thing she'll respond to is him laying siege to her, trying to force her into a talk or a confrontation or a reconciliation. Just now, though, for the first time, I felt hopeful for the two of them— that eventually they'll work it out.'

'Me, too,' he agreed. 'What does that make us?'

'Optimists?' she suggested dryly.

'More than that…'

'What, Harry?'

But he only shrugged, and silence fell all through the empty rooms of the practice. It was the first time they'd been alone together since Sunday afternoon, and she was almost painfully aware of it.

She didn't know what to do. Leave? They were both ready—overdue, in fact—to lock up for the day. And yet the last thing she wanted was just to drift off, as if they had nothing to do with each other and nothing to say. What on earth had happened since Sunday?

'Well…'

The word dropped from her lips almost without her volition, and she found herself bustling off down the corridor to check the windows in each room and make sure that everything was switched off. Behind her, she could hear Harry setting the answering machine for the weekend.

When she arrived back in the waiting-room he was at the front door, holding it open for her. She was just about to brush past him, steeling herself against the reaction to his closeness which she knew was inevitable, then they both heard tottering, hesitant footsteps just outside, punctuated by the staccato knock of a stick on cement.

'Hello…' Harry muttered. 'Who's this?'

'Oh, Doctor, thank goodness!'

It was Irene MacInerney, and she was far too agitated and upset to think of flirting with Dr Jones today, although as usual she was very smartly and neatly dressed.

'What is it, Mrs MacInerney?' Harry asked, but then he and Rebecca both saw the problem.

The ninety-six-year-old's lower calf was bleeding profusely, and the fragile, almost transparent skin was torn back like a strip of soggy paper. Blood had soaked through the knee-high stocking she'd been wearing, which was now rolled down to her ankle.

'I'm a silly, *silly* old thing,' she was saying, close to tears. 'I got up on a step stool to try and reach my top cupboard—I should have waited for my son to come and do it for me—

and I had one of my dizzies and fell, and my shoe heel must have scraped my ankle and look at me!'

Harry had already bounded down the steps to reach her, taking her elbow and putting an arm around her shoulders so he could pilot her up the steps.

'Don't go scolding yourself and getting upset, Mrs Mac,' he ordered her gently. 'Just tell me, is anything else hurting? Your hip or your thigh?'

'No…'

'And you can walk quite normally?'

'Apart from the trail of blood I'm leaving at every step. People will think someone's been attacked! Oh, I'm *so* silly!'

Lucky, though. She hadn't broken any bones, which was almost a miracle given her age. Rebecca held the door open and Harry got their patient safely into a treatment room then helped her to lie down while Rebecca got the equipment they would need to tape and dress the leg.

In many ways it wasn't as bad as it looked. If a young person had produced that much blood, stitches would probably have been needed, but this was quite a shallow scrape. On the other hand, Mrs MacInerney's skin was so very fine and fragile that the job of stretching it back into position and taping the wound closed was both delicate and time-consuming.

Really, it was well within the capabilities of a single doctor, but somehow neither Harry nor Rebecca thought of suggesting to the other that they should leave, and Rebecca happily took on the role of assistant, cutting the tape to the length Harry required and distracting Mrs MacInerney with conversation.

Meanwhile, she was badly distracted herself—by the sight of Harry at work over the injury. She hadn't seen him like this before, so focused and careful. How could those strong fingers be so delicate and meticulous? He was doing a superb job…as he'd done last weekend with his hands in a very different context.

How can I possibly think about that *now*? Rebecca scolded herself.

'I've spoilt your evening,' Mrs MacInerney was saying. 'Oh, I'm such a nuisance!'

'You haven't spoiled anything, Mrs Mac,' Harry said soothingly, then added, 'OK, Rebecca, about five centimetres, thank you.'

'Here you go.'

Their fingers brushed and their eyes met. Rebecca felt heat rise in her face at once and thought in despair, Oh, *why* does my face give so much away? I should start wearing a mask when I'm with him! She knew he'd seen the colour in her cheeks.

'There's a lot of evening left yet,' Harry said in a significant way. Looking at Mrs MacInerney. Speaking to Rebecca.

She flushed and dropped her gaze. She *wasn't* going to take suggestive comments from him when things were so unclear between them. She definitely wasn't going to take such things in the middle of a delicate piece of skin repair.

'One more piece?' she said.

'Should about do it.' He echoed her own professional tone, but as she looked down at the spool of tape she was aware of his gaze, drifting to her at every spare moment. 'Now, you're up to date on your tetanus shots, aren't you, Mrs Mac?' he said next.

'Yes, because of the silly cut I got in the garden, back when my daughter-in-law gave me the New Guinea impatiens plants.'

'OK, yes, I remember. That's good, but I'm going to put you on an antibiotic because if this got infected it could get way out of control, and I want you back on Tuesday so we can look at the dressing. I'm afraid it's going to be slow to heal.'

'Well, I'll just have to resign myself to seeing a lot of you, then, won't I, Dr Jones?'

'Aha!' He pounced on the flirting tone. 'You're starting to feel better! Now, is there someone who can come over and look after you for the evening?'

'My son. He was coming anyway. He's probably on his way. He's very good to me!'

'I know he is,' Harry answered.

This was what allowed Mrs MacInerney to live alone successfully, and she was very appreciative and proud of the loving support she received from each of her three children.

'We'd better walk you back, then,' Harry said.

'Could I take my other knee-high off first?' Mrs MacInerney said. 'I don't want to look strange.'

'Rebecca, would you mind writing out that script for her while we start off? Don't want to rush things! Your dad's...er...been telling me he doesn't think rushing things is a good idea,' he finished significantly.

'Has he?' she said rather huskily, understanding. Oh, *Dad*... She added helplessly, 'You know, Harry, Dad's not *always* right! He can be—'

'Clever, distinguished, generous...'

'All that,' she agreed, confused now.

'And dead wrong about his daughter?'

'Oh, *dead* wrong about his daughter,' Rebecca agreed, then looked at Mrs MacInerney. What on earth was she making of this cryptic yet patently significant exchange? Fortunately she was still absorbed in rolling down her knee-high and replacing her shoe on the uninjured leg.

It was another ten minutes before she was safely seated on her couch with her bandaged leg propped on a footstool, and this was the sight that greeted her son John when he walked through the front door.

'Oh, Mum, no! What have you done?'

Harry and Rebecca left their elderly patient to tell the story, after Harry had told her firmly, 'None of this "silly" business, OK? You'll know next time that the step stool isn't a good idea. Mr MacInerney, maybe it needs to live at your place from now on.'

'Sounds that way!' her son said.

'And now…' Harry said ominously to Rebecca as soon as they'd regained the street, along which a fresh sea breeze blew to cool the hot golden evening.

'Yes?' she returned, as impatient as he was. 'Dad's been meddling, hasn't he?'

'He had a long talk to me on Monday.'

'I gathered that.'

'He'd guessed…'

'About the—?'

'Weekend,' he finished with a nod. It seemed entirely natural for them to complete each other's sentences like this. 'He didn't…uh…threaten me with anything terrible.' A smile played lightly on his face. 'Though I think he wanted to!'

Rebecca's face burned. 'Right,' she said faintly.

'But as I…er…implied a few minutes ago, he did suggest that it would be advisable if I didn't rush you into anything…and if I made absolutely sure of what we both felt, before putting you in any position where you could possibly be hurt.'

'Oh, God, it's too late for that,' she muttered.

He misunderstood. 'Too *late*?' he rasped. 'What do you mean? That David you were out with when I rang the other night…?' The pained, jealous ring in his voice was unmistakable.

'No, Harry!' she said frantically, taking an urgent pace towards him. They could have touched now with only the tiniest effort, but they didn't. 'Too late to make sure I couldn't be hurt,' she clarified. 'I— You already have a terrible power to hurt me, Harry,' she admitted honestly, the colour flaring once again in her face.

Oh, God, it was terrible once you'd slept with a man, and she'd known it would be like this for her. The searing truths from inside her heart could only come tumbling forth fully formed into words. She finished, 'I think I've been a mess of about a hundred different painful feelings since the day we met.'

'So let's get this quite clear,' Harry said cautiously. '*Do* you need time, Rebecca?'

'No!' she almost shouted. 'No, I do not need time! I know exactly how I feel about you, and what I want.'

'You love me.' It wasn't a question. His confidence might have seemed arrogant if the relief vibrating in his tone hadn't been so naked and joyous.

'Yes.'

'Then, if I take a leaf out of Marcus Gaines's book and ask you to marry me *now*, when we've known each other for less than three months, you're saying it won't be too soon?'

His voice seared into her ear as he took her in his arms and ran his hands with possessive heat over the curves that had writhed under his touch just days ago.

'Oh, Harry, I'm not a patient person,' she whispered, closing her eyes and then gasping as his lips trailed down her throat then moved upwards to find her mouth. 'Dad should have known that…'

'Neither am I when it comes to you,' he growled. 'Nor am I very good at keeping my feelings to myself. Marcus and Grace scared me today. Badly. And then I saw your reaction the moment we touched. Just like mine… It's been such hell, holding back this week. Coming on top of Sunday when we said goodbye in the doctors' car park and you didn't turn back to wave…'

'Oh, Harry, because I was feeling so overwhelmed,' she told him. 'And so scared myself that I hadn't allowed enough time, that I'd dived in at the deep end too soon. I'd always known it would happen, you see, once I reached that ultimate closeness with a man, and when it *did* it was even more powerful than I'd imagined.'

'Oh, was it *ever*?' he said fervently, and her insides coiled with secret rapture at the knowledge that it had been just as special and powerful for him.

'So I felt I had to start putting on the brakes. You saying goodbye to me that day at all was so hard, like being pushed out into the cold after basking for hours in front of a warm fire.'

'Marry me, then, Rebecca,' he said urgently. 'Promise me now that you will so that we both know exactly where we stand.'

'I will, Harry. You know that...'

They didn't speak again for quite some time, then Harry said, 'Can I come over for dinner, then? I want to put your poor father out of his misery, tell him that he can stop having those shotgun wedding nightmares of his. It's going to make a nice change from the past few months, not having to worry that my attitude towards you is going to ruin my professional relationship with your dad.'

'Was your attitude to me ever really that negative?' she asked, with a strong inkling that she knew the answer to this question now.

'Rebecca,' he confirmed, deeply serious, 'from the moment I saw you in that chic little pink Chanel suit—'

'*What?*'

'The pink towel ensemble.'

She laughed. 'I was picturing it as Donna Karan...'

'Either way, it was obvious you had exceptionally good taste in towels, and from that moment my attitude towards you was so dangerously *positive* that it completely panicked me about the future of the practice. On top of that, I could see at once that you and your father had some preconceptions to get rid of where each other was concerned. Now I'll be in a perfect position to set you both straight!'

'Smug, aren't you?'

'I think men usually are,' he whispered, 'when they've just got what they most want in the world.'

He nuzzled her nose with his, then brushed her lips, coaxing them to part before covering her mouth with his.

'You were right to worry about the future of the practice,' she said after several blissful minutes. 'It's not going to look very stable to the outside eye, is it, when the practice goes from being Irwin, Gaines, Jones and Irwin to Irwin, Gaines, Jones and Jones within a matter of months?'

'Not very stable at all,' Harry agreed unsteadily. He was finding it increasingly difficult to have a rational conversation, with Rebecca's lithe, curved and scented body pressed invitingly against him and the sun pouring molten gold into her living hair. She tasted like heaven. 'But somehow I think when patients hear the reason for it they'll understand.'

My very worst fears have been realised, he thought hazily and happily. She *did* change the whole balance of my working relationship with Marshall, and it's the best thing that ever happened to me.

'Did you tell your father what time you'd be home tonight?' he managed to ask.

'For dinner,' she said, then frowned. 'Didn't you want to come over, too?'

'I've changed my mind,' he answered. 'Would he object if you rang and said you were going out with me?'

'He wouldn't object,' she assured him. 'We'll tell him our news tomorrow, then?'

'Sounds good.'

'And what time should I tell him I'll be home?' She knew the answer already. Her eyes were sparkling wickedly. They'd already turned towards the beach. Their cars were parked in the opposite direction, but that didn't matter.

'Late,' Harry said firmly. 'Very, *very* late!'

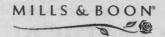

MILLS & BOON®

*Makes
any time
special*

Copyright © Harlequin Enterprises Limited 1997
All rights reserved

**Enjoy a romantic novel from
Mills & Boon®**

Presents...™   *Enchanted*™   *Temptation*™

Historical Romance™   *Medical Romance*™

MILLS & BOON®

MEDICAL ROMANCE™

PRACTICALLY PERFECT by Caroline Anderson

Surgeon Connie Wright found locum G.P. Patrick Durrant deeply attractive and his small son Edward soon found a place in her heart. But Patrick would be moving on and Connie would be returning to London…

TAKE TWO BABIES… by Josie Metcalfe

Maddie's ex-husband had kidnapped her daughter and she was distraught. When Dr William Ward was so supportive, Maddie knew this man was for her…

TENDER LIAISON by Joanna Neil

Dr Daniel Maitland doesn't believe Dr Emma Barnes will stay in his practice—nor does he believe Emma when she says he has a lot of love to give!

A HUGS-AND-KISSES FAMILY by Meredith Webber
Bundles of Joy

Dr Angus McLeod had never stopped loving Jen, his only thought to woo and win her all over again. Discovering Jen was pregnant was *such* a shock!

Available from 1st October 1999

Available at most branches of WH Smith, Tesco, Asda, Martins, Borders, Easons, Volume One/James Thin and most good paperback bookshops

MILLS & BOON®

Next Month's Romance Titles

♡

Each month you can choose from a wide variety of
romance novels from Mills & Boon®. Below are the new
titles to look out for next month from the Presents...™
and Enchanted™ series.

Presents...™

A RELUCTANT MISTRESS	Robyn Donald
THE MARRIAGE RESOLUTION	Penny Jordan
THE FINAL SEDUCTION	Sharon Kendrick
THE REVENGE AFFAIR	Susan Napier
THE HIRED HUSBAND	Kate Walker
THE MILLIONAIRE AFFAIR	Sophie Weston
THE BABY VERDICT	Cathy Williams
THE IMPATIENT GROOM	Sara Wood

Enchanted™

THE DADDY DILEMMA	Kate Denton
AND MOTHER MAKES THREE	Liz Fielding
TO CLAIM A WIFE	Susan Fox
THE BABY WISH	Myrna Mackenzie
MARRYING A MILLIONAIRE	Laura Martin
THE HUSBAND CAMPAIGN	Barbara McMahon
TEMPTING A TYCOON	Leigh Michaels
MAIL-ORDER MARRIAGE	Margaret Way

On sale from 1st October 1999

H1 9909

*Available at most branches of WH Smith, Tesco, Asda,
Martins, Borders, Easons, Volume One/James Thin
and most good paperback bookshops*

2 BOOKS
AND A SURPRISE GIFT!

We would like to take this opportunity to thank you for reading this Mills & Boon® book by offering you the chance to take TWO more specially selected titles from the Medical Romance™ series absolutely FREE! We're also making this offer to introduce you to the benefits of the Reader Service™—

    ★ FREE home delivery   ★ FREE gifts and competitions
    ★ FREE monthly Newsletter   ★ Exclusive Reader Service discounts
           ★ Books available before they're in the shops

Accepting these FREE books and gift places you under no obligation to buy; you may cancel at any time, even after receiving your free shipment. Simply complete your details below and return the entire page to the address below. *You don't even need a stamp!*

YES! Please send me 2 free Medical Romance books and a surprise gift. I understand that unless you hear from me, I will receive 4 superb new titles every month for just £2.40 each, postage and packing free. I am under no obligation to purchase any books and may cancel my subscription at any time. The free books and gift will be mine to keep in any case.

M9EC

Ms/Mrs/Miss/Mr ....Initials ....
                                                    BLOCK CAPITALS PLEASE

Surname ....

Address ....

....

....Postcode ....

Send this whole page to:
UK: FREEPOST CN81, Croydon, CR9 3WZ
EIRE: PO Box 4546, Kilcock, County Kildare (stamp required)

Offer valid in UK and Eire only and not available to current Reader Service subscribers to this series. We reserve the right to refuse an application and applicants must be aged 18 years or over. Only one application per household. Terms and prices subject to change without notice. Offer expires 31st March 2000. As a result of this application, you may receive further offers from Harlequin Mills & Boon Limited and other carefully selected companies. If you would prefer not to share in this opportunity please write to The Data Manager at the address above.

Mills & Boon is a registered trademark owned by Harlequin Mills & Boon Limited.
Medical Romance is being used as a trademark.

MILLS & BOON®

Medicine and Marriage
Southshore has it all.

NEW

From Lilian Darcy

If you have enjoyed
Her Passion for Dr Jones

Look out for no. 2
The Courage to Say Yes

Available from 3rd December